Marc could see the stunned driver drop his microphone. The next thing he saw was a bright flash licking from the barrel of a pistol. Marc returned fire with the Uzi, the subgun spitting 9mm death at the Coastal rig.

The driver panicked, floored the accelerator, and his rig leaped ahead. Carl stomped his own accelerator and brought the rig up to the rear wheels of the Coastal tractor. Bullets slammed into the windshield just over Carl's head and flew harmlessly into the headliner of the cab.

"Take it up two more feet," Marc shouted.

The Kenworth moved forward, both rigs dangerously gaining speed. Marc leaned from the window and fired out the Uzi with bursts of flames licking into the night. The flying death pellets found their mark—a geyser of steam suddenly gyrated from the front of the outlaw tractor. . . .

Bantam Books by Bob Ham:

Overload #1: Personal War
Overload #2: The Wrath

OVERLOAD, Book 3

HIGHWAY WARRIORS

Bob Ham

BANTAM BOOKS
NEW YORK • TORONTO • LONDON • SYDNEY • AUCKLAND

HIGHWAY WARRIORS

A Bantam Book / September 1989

ISBN 0-553-28148-8

Bantam Books are published by Bantam Books, a division of Bantam Doubleday Dell Publishing Group, Inc. Its trademark, consisting of the words "Bantam Books" and the portrayal of a rooster, is Registered in U.S. Patent and Trademark Office and in other countries. Marca Registrada. Bantam Books, 666 Fifth Avenue, New York, New York 10103.

For Bob Robison and Greg Tobin . . . who believed

Never give out while there is Hope; but Hope not beyond Reason, for that shews more Desire than Judgment.

—WILLIAM PENN

———————————————————————

I don't regret what I've done. All I seek is undiluted, real justice. The ones who harm innocents must always be held accountable. Where society's system of accountability fails, I won't.

—MARC LEE

ACKNOWLEDGMENTS

My special thanks to two very knowledgeable friends: Butch Smith, fellow radio amateur, and Shipley Landis, electronics whiz, both of The Nashville Network engineering section. Without the assistance of these two guys, the high-tech design of Marc and Carl's overroad rig in this story and subsequent stories would have been much more difficult. It is by the trusted assistance of these two friends that Marc Lee and Carl Browne will ride the highways of America with an advanced communications capability that challenges the penetrating fringes of modern technology. In a society that demands newer and better ways to communicate and transfer pertinent data, Marc and Carl will help break new unscathed ground for land-mobile technology and overroad transportation. Any technical errors that have occurred or might occur are certainly mine and not theirs.

Thanks, guys. I owe you one. . . .

Brentwood, Tennessee
October 1988

CHAPTER ONE

The huge forklift lowered the last steel-encapsulated canister onto the Strick flatbed trailer. The cylindrical canisters were almost four feet long and two feet in diameter. They resembled marker buoys found on most lakes. But unlike the navigational aides, the units contained lethal levels of strontium-90 and cesium-137 . . . radioactive isotopes.

Workmen in white lab jackets, carrying clipboards and making notes, swarmed around the overroad rig. A team of packaging specialists boarded the trailer and started securing heavy rubber-coated steel chains. They ran the chains from each side of the trailer and fastened them along the sides of the canisters. Once the packaging specialists were satisfied with their work, they disembarked and disappeared.

Artlie Anders watched the workers, and when they were finished he climbed aboard the trailer and double-checked their work. It was Monday morning and he knew workers weren't always at their best on Monday mornings. Anders was an articulate man in his mid-forties who demanded perfection where his cargo was concerned. He had a thick crop of black hair combed in a wave toward the back of his head. He was stocky and as firm as a fresh-picked grapefruit. Anders usually smiled and when he did,

1

a half-dozen gold-capped teeth shone in his mouth. He was proud of them, so he smiled whenever he could.

Anders decided the packaging technicians were thorough and the chains were effectively secured to the canisters. Even if he were unfortunate enough to crash the rig, the huge drumlike titanium steel transportation devices should withstand the ride. But as an independent trucker running his own rig and carving out his own slice of bread and butter, it never hurt to be extra cautious. Anders had learned long ago that nuclear regulatory boards were hell on technicalities, and besides that, the run made him a nice living. He always went the extra mile to be sure he maintained the government contract. And in balancing those assurances, he knew one screwup and it could all be over. So caution was his second nature.

Anders double-checked his manifest. There were supposed to be twelve high-security canisters of nuclear waste product. He counted them on the trailer once more, and there were indeed twelve. Each was labeled with the proper decal and radioactive insignia. Anders covered the canisters with a blue tarp and tied it off on the flatbed's tie-downs. He went to the cab of his Autocar and found the Interstate Commerce Commission placards behind the seat. Choosing the ones indicating radioactive materials, he placed the yellow and black warning signs around the trailer in metal holders.

Anders finished the placard placement and made a quick walk around the rig for a final prerun inspection. Everything appeared secure and roadworthy. He signed the necessary documents and headed off for the open road with a load of nuclear waste consigned to an obscure government facility just outside of Grass Lake, California. The small town of Grass Lake was the least likely candidate for a top-secret nuclear dumping ground. Anders felt a sense of pride in his knowledge of the facility, since few, if any, people outside of the military or the Nuclear Regulatory Commission knew of the facility's existence. But then, he'd earned that pride by not only winning the exclusive government contract, but also passing the necessary security clearances required to consummate the agreement.

Anders turned up the volume on his CB radio on the instrument console as he left the Nellis Nuclear Testing Site in western Nevada. He slid a cassette tape into the player mounted under the CB and settled in for the long overroad run.

Several hours passed as Anders ran U.S. 95 North to Interstate 80. He headed west on I-80 to Interstate 5 in Sacramento, then went north on I-5. He stopped at a truckstop near Red Bluff, grabbed a meal, and refueled the rig.

Anders saw the rest area sign north of Red Bluff and realized he had consumed one cup too many of truckstop coffee before he left Red Bluff. He eased the rig off the highway and into the parking area, then made a mad dash for the restroom. Once again comfortable, he rinsed his face in cool water and went back to the rig. It was as he reached for the door handle after he unlocked the cab door that he first saw them—three Asian men surrounding him. Anders kept his hand poised on the door handle. His knees felt slightly weak, so he didn't speak. He simply froze.

"Please step down," the man nearest him said. He had coal-black hair and dark, penetrating eyes. His Asian skin accented the black clothing he was wearing. What Anders noticed most were the man's yellow teeth.

"What do you guys want?" Anders asked nervously.

"Your cargo," the man to his right said. He was taller and thinner than the man who had spoken first, but he too was dressed in black.

"You got to be shittin' me," Anders said. "All this stuff is good for is makin' you glow in the dark."

The third man, behind Anders, moved in between the first two. He gave Anders a hard, piercing stare and then smiled.

"We can think of a few other things to do with it. Step down now and perhaps we will decide not to kill you," he said. This man was also tall and lean, but heavier than the other two. He was older—mid-forties, Anders guessed. But like the first two Asian men, he spoke perfect English.

"Who the hell are you?" Anders asked as he felt his knees getting weaker by the second.

"For whatever good it will do you, in my homeland I am called Mori Osamu," the man said, his smile still creasing his face. "We mean no harm to you. We want only your cargo. Please get out of the way."

"Sorry, Mori Osamu, I can't do that," Anders said, and he leapt for the man. Osamu sidestepped and with the grace of a master slapped a full heel of his hand chop into Anders' collarbone. The bone snapped with little resistance. Anders fell to the ground in intense pain.

"I too am sorry," Osamu said as he stood over Anders and smiled, a black automatic pistol in his hands. Anders recognized the oversized barrel as a silencer, and his heart raced despite the pain. His eyebrows tightened and his face froze in a mixture of horror and bewilderment.

Anders felt an intense burning in his chest; but he didn't hear the shot. Then he felt it again and again. Through fading eyes, he saw Osamu standing over him. The Asian's face was split wide with a smile of pleasure. His teeth shined as he held the handgun at arm's length. As the last light of life escaped from his eyes, Anders thought what a nice gold incisor Osamu had.

———

A thin ray of light from the Thursday morning sun penetrated the narrow window slit and settled in on Marc

Lee's rugged face, causing him to stir. He moved slightly in the tiny bed, stretching his muscles and opening his eyes, then pulled the blanket aside and sat upright. He put both hands behind his neck, stretched, and ran his fingers through his thick black hair.

Marc stared blankly at the window. It was small, only four inches wide and maybe four feet high. The glass was over an inch thick and distorted the sunlight, refracting the rays into multiple slivered rainbows. On the other side of the high-security glass lay the free world—his freedom. But at the moment, the other side of the glass might just as well be another planet in some far-off galaxy.

Marc's shoulders hurt with residual pain from a bullet that had passed through him just days before in a bloody shoot-out with outlaw bikers in a tunnel near Gatlinburg, Tennessee. It was for a purpose he believed in that he had risked his life and lost his freedom. But then, Marc Lee was the kind of man who would risk everything for something he believed in. He and Carl Browne, his military partner, friend, and second-in-command for the elite U.S. Army Delta Force, had squashed forever the appendages of evil that had wrapped their tentacles around his father's trucking business in Dallas, Texas. But Dallas was a world away from the high-security detaining cell holding him at Quantico, Virginia.

Marc's thoughts flew out the window . . . to freedom. To Dallas. He had lost more than his freedom in the war with the mob. His mother and uncle were killed by mobsters when the Lee family home was blown into eternity. Marcus Lee, Marc's father, lay unconscious somewhere in Dallas. And that disturbed the rugged Delta Warrior, because right now he didn't know for sure where his father was. Before he was arrested, his father had been in a safe-room designed for witness protection and used by law enforcement agencies. But Marc had heard that his lifelong friend and police contact, Brittin Crain, was also in FBI custody, charged with being an accessory to Marc and Carl.

The agents interviewing Marc had been friendly, yet all business. They had treated him well, but he feared the worst was yet to come. He knew he had to find a way out. He had to know about his father and Jill Lanier, the blue-eyed blond he had recently fallen in love with all over again. Jill worked for Leeco Freight Lines, Marcus Lee's firm, until the mob virtually destroyed it with fire and caused Marc to seek final retribution. And that was why he was in the detaining cell: He had delivered his own brand of cleansing justice to the perpetrators of the crimes against his family and Leeco. But the finale had taken an unexpected twist and he and Carl now faced dozens of criminal charges for their actions.

Marc looked around the room. It was small, but clean. There was a sink with hot and cold running water, a commode, and a bunk. Three of the interior walls were concrete painted military gray. The window that allowed the sun to enter his prison was on the exterior wall. The fourth wall wasn't a wall at all, it was one-inch-diameter steel bars.

The captured warrior walked to the window and looked out. The only view of freedom he had was rooftops and blacktop surrounding the impoundment.

The very thought of freedom led Marc to Leeco Freight Lines and one of the reasons he was in such serious legal trouble. It was for the sake of Leeco he had risked it all. And although he had won the war, he had lost a major battle. Marc suddenly realized the importance of freedom, and he knew how a caged animal accustomed to the wild must feel when it was restricted by force. But now he wondered what would happen to Leeco. And for the first time in his life, he longed for the open road and an eighteen-wheeler. He reaffirmed a decision he had made some days earlier, prior to his arrest. When he walked away from the legal maze that awaited him, he would head to the open road. He would leave the Army and take care of Leeco until his father was physically able to assume control again. He would roll eighteen wheels across America and let his life settle down. It was a firm decision. But first he had to gain his freedom.

The mechanical steel-barred door slid open behind him. A man in a tan and green uniform stepped in holding a breakfast tray. "Here's breakfast, Major. You'd better eat hearty. Agent Harrison called about fifteen minutes ago and he's coming for you and Captain Browne in thirty minutes."

"What's the occasion this time?" Marc asked.

"Beats me. He just told us to have you ready to go."

"More interviews I suppose," Marc said disgustedly. "Damn, I've already told them everything I know. Do they ever quit?"

"Yep," the jailer answered. "When they get what they want."

"They may get a lot more than they bargained for." Marc forced a smile. "Much more."

———

Carl was already in the helicopter when the guards helped Marc inside. Marc ducked his head and shielded his face against the rotor draft as he climbed into the Bell Jet Ranger. It was difficult to move, with the body shackles and handcuffs. The leg chains made climbing very hard, so the guards had been forced to push Marc into the chopper. He settled into a seat and looked around. He saw his friend for the first time since their arrest in Tennessee.

"Well, brother," Carl said once Marc was comfortably seated, "looks like we got ourselves a hell of a mess this time."

"Yeah," Marc said. "I'm sorry I brought you into all this."

"Don't be. I'm a big boy. I make my own decisions, and my decision was to help you and your family. I don't regret that."

"I hope you don't when this is all over."

"I hope we both don't," Carl said.

The chopper lifted off and Marc looked at FBI Agent Harvey Harrison. It was the stone-faced Harrison who had arrested them in Gatlinburg. The tall, middle-aged man had sat silently watching Marc and Carl.

"Mr. Harrison, not that it's any of my business, but just where the hell are you taking us?" Marc asked.

"To talk with someone," the hard-faced FBI agent said.

"I seem to recall something about Constitutional rights—attorneys, and all that. Are we so bad you've decided to circumvent our rights to counsel?"

The agent didn't answer for a long moment. He stared at Marc, then at Carl as the helicopter ate the sky across northern Virginia. "Are you men as good as General Rogers says you are?" he asked abruptly.

"Better," Carl said confidently. "The good general only sees the good side of us. I don't think he's ever seen us when we're mad."

FBI Agent Harrison stared again, his jaw jutting and his face void of meaningful expression.

"Where are we going?" Marc asked.

"Like I said, someone wants to speak with you in private," the cold FBI man said.

Marc turned away and looked out the window as the structures on the ground below became tiny dots moving swiftly past the airborne bird in rapid succession. He noticed the position of the sun . . . behind them. This time of day, that meant the chopper was flying west. And west eliminated a trip to Washington, D.C. Marc watched the dense ground clutter of houses, buildings, and cars disappear. Below them now was open farmland dotted by an occasional barn or farmhouse.

"Don't tell me; let me guess," Marc said. "We're going to the presidential war command center in the mountains?"

Agent Harrison looked at Marc and almost forced a smile. "Not exactly."

"Don't you get it, brother?" Carl chided. "He's taking us out in the boonies to blow us away. These turkeys think we aren't telling them something."

"Not exactly," Harrison said, and this time he smiled an indecipherable smile.

"You're just a wealth of information," Marc said, and he faced the window again as the helicopter steadily consumed the northern Virginia sky.

The chopper had been flying west less than an hour when Marc noticed a radical change in the topography. The land was becoming more hilly, and soon a mountain range appeared. The chopper flew directly over the mountains and made a course correction. The pilot now had the ship flying west-southwest. Marc mentally calculated their position and projected that the rugged mountains were the Blue Ridge chain. His mind slipped back a few weeks to the personal war he and Carl had waged with Rafaello Segalini's mob. It had been in the Blue Ridge Mountains that he had found Carl and they had destroyed a cocaine repackaging facility used by Segalini for a major distribution point. He and Carl had left Segalini's snow-covered mountain farm in bloody, blazing ruins. Now Marc wondered if the FBI man had some reason to take them back to the scene of their retribution.

The chopper continued across the top of the mountains. Marc watched the landscape sweep by for another twenty minutes.

"Where are we going, Mr. Harrison?" Marc asked again, breaking the silence inside the helicopter.

"That's really worrying you, isn't it?" Harrison said. "All right, then. We're close, so I think there would be no harm in telling you. We're going to a highly secret place in the George Washington National Forest. It lies high in the mountains and it's accessible only by helicopter or a damn good four-wheel drive vehicle. It lies just outside of a little community called Sherando."

"You're a wealth of information," Marc said. "Does this place have a name?"

"It sure does. The locals call it *Where They Took The Dirt Out*. It's a huge clearing, probably forty or more acres, cleared by the Forest Service to get fill-dirt for an earthen dam for winter flood control. The clearing lies below the dam, which was constructed in the late sixties. It serves as a water source for wildlife and manages to control potential flooding when the rains come. There's some great native trout fishing in the lake's feeder stream."

"What does a flood control dam have to do with Carl and me?" Marc asked.

"As I said, it's virtually inaccessible and it doesn't present a security problem," Harrison said.

"Are we that *bad*?" Carl asked.

Agent Harrison didn't respond for a long moment. Instead, he looked at Carl, then at Marc, as if he were etching their images into the deep recesses of his mind for permanent instant retrieval. His previously stone-etched face slowly mellowed and the stone was replaced with lines of sincerity and genuine concern. "For the sake of this country and everything it stands for, I certainly hope you are."

CHAPTER TWO

The Bell Jet Ranger flew due west and suddenly banked hard left. As the pilot leaned the aircraft into the bank, they made a swooping pass over a mountain crest and descended into the valley below. Marc stared out the window. Behind the chopper, to the northeast, the town of Sherando appeared as little more than a fleeting wide spot in the lone roadway that wove its way through the mountains. Below, on the forest floor, was a large clearing just below an earthen dam. Harrison's description had been accurate. The lake backed by the dam looked to be thirty or forty acres. Its shores were densely wooded and the water was crystal clear. The lake and clearing lay in one of numerous tributary valleys that separated the high mountain ridges like long spiny tentacles reaching out into the George Washington National Forest.

The clearing was barren except for the four-wheel drive vehicles dotting its center. Marc counted six of the off-road machines. There were also men—many men—and they were all dressed in fall-pattern camouflage or TreBark.

"We have clearance, Mr. Harrison," the pilot said over the intercom headphones.

"Thanks, Lou. Take her in." Harrison responded.

The chopper made one more pass over the clearing in a full banking circle. The pilot eased the mighty Bell toward the clearing, remaining a safe distance away from the parked vehicles.

"Harrison, if you're bringing us out here on a one-way trip, you've sure gone to a lot of trouble," Marc said coldly.

FBI Agent Harrison looked at Marc. His face resumed its normally cold, blank look and he didn't speak.

The pilot landed the Bell Jet with textbook precision. He cut the engine and the rotor started decelerating. Agent Harrison slid the door open and Marc found himself staring into more cold faces. The helicopter was surrounded by the men he had seen from the air. Every man he saw was brandishing a fully automatic weapon.

"Okay, gentlemen," Harrison said. "Time to get out."

"Shit, man. I don't think I like the smell of this," Carl said as he stood from his seat.

"Be cool, Captain," Marc said.

"Out," Agent Harrison said, motioning with his right hand toward the open chopper door. He waited for Marc and Carl to jump to the ground before he followed. Once outside, the air was cool despite the high sun.

Marc looked around the clearing, mentally assessing his situation. All he could see in any direction were high forested mountain peaks and men with automatic weapons. One of the vehicles near the center of the clearing, a black Jeep Cherokee, had its engine running. The windows on the idling Cherokee were darkly tinted and visibility into it was impossible.

"This way," Harrison said and he motioned toward the vehicles.

The men walked toward the running Cherokee. They were flanked on every side by camo-clad men holding Uzis, M-16s, and Ingrams at ready.

"What is this shit, Harrison?" Carl asked.

"You'll find out in just a few seconds," Harrison said without breaking his stride.

The group reached the black Cherokee. The rear passenger door opened and out stepped General A. J. Rogers III, commander of Delta Force. The elderly general appeared to be still a bit overweight, and when he stepped to the ground his cheeks shook in rhythm with his steps.

"Major. Captain," Rogers said. "I trust you have had a pleasant journey?"

"What is this, General, the latest in military discipline?" Marc asked testily.

Settle down, Major. Before this is all over today, I think you'll understand. More importantly, I think you'll concur. I have someone who wants to speak with you." Rogers turned back toward the Jeep.

A man in his mid-fifties appeared at the open door. He had a red-tinged fair complexion with graying hair. He appeared fit and trim, but worried. He was dressed in a 10-X hunting coat complete with twelve-gauge shotgun shells in elastic holders at the side pockets. As the man stepped from the vehicle, Marc noticed his hunting boots showed signs of much usage. He extended a hand to Marc and shook his manacled hand.

"Major, nice to see you again. I wish it was under better circumstances," the man said.

"Mr. President, I too would prefer different circumstances."

"And you must be Captain Browne," the president said as he took Carl's hand. "I am pleased to meet you. I've heard a lot about you, Captain."

"Yes, sir," Carl replied as he stood at attention out of habit. "And I, you—sir."

"Mr. Harrison, take these handcuffs and shackles off of these men. I think everything will be all right," the president said.

Harrison didn't answer, but he immediately removed the restraining devices.

Marc and Carl flexed their hands and wrists. They stretched their arms and moved their legs to get full circulation moving again.

"Thanks, Mr. President," Marc said, and the tall man simply shook his head and smiled.

"A.J., Marc, Carl, let's take a walk. I want to talk with the three of you alone." The president moved away from the armed men and the Jeep. He walked slowly until he was out of hearing range of anyone except the men by his side. Then he stopped abruptly and faced the two Delta Warriors. "Major Lee, Captain Browne, I'm going to get straight to the point of this meeting. You men have some potentially serious problems. You have broken more laws than I can count. Both of you could face prison for as long as you live. Personally, I think you both have too much knowledge, training, and ability to waste away like that. It would be shameful to allow your various talents to stagnate. I'm not even sure our society has a facility that could contain men like you if you ever decided you just didn't want to stay anymore. Your arrest was on my specific order. A.J. and the others had nothing to do with it. They were simply carrying out my directives. You have my apology for your inconvenience. How's your arm, Marc?"

"Fine, sir. It's still stiff, but in a few days it'll be as good as new."

Carl stood silent and wide-eyed, not believing he was actually in the company of the president of the United States.

"Good, I'm glad to hear that. I trust, then, the medical treatment was to your satisfaction?"

"No complaints," Marc replied.

"Good. I'll continue. I am in a position to wipe your slate clean and I want to do that. I happen to think, as A.J. does, that you two men are the very best frontline defense this country has. You're both damned good and I want to help, but I have a problem too. As you can see, we are meeting in a strange place. I used to come here trout fishing when I was a junior Senator. The beauty of this place called *Where They Took The Dirt Out* is simple: Few people know about it, especially the press. It wouldn't be good for the president of the United States to be seen in the company of fugitive criminals, no matter who or what you really are. That's one of my problems. The other is, I want something from you in return."

"Like what?" Marc asked.

"Your help at cleaning up this country," the gray-haired statesman said.

"I thought that's why we have police and FBI and things like that," Carl said.

"Men, you two accomplished in less than two weeks what the entire federal system couldn't do in five years. You broke a major leg of organized crime. You completely destroyed a massive drug distribution empire. And you did it in two weeks."

"Don't pat us on the back too soon, Mr. President. That war was personal and we didn't start it," Marc said.

"I know that. I know everything about your adventures. From time to time, there are, shall we say, *problems,* that surface which would require your expertise. Are you interested."

"Depends," Marc said.

"On what?" the president asked.

"On what the rules are," Marc replied.

"The rules are simple. You go into selected situations with only one purpose and intent—to win!"

"What about laws and reporters, stuff like that?" Carl asked.

"You go in, you win, and you're gone. No one is the wiser. You get caught and the federal government knows nothing of your existence."

"Go on," Marc said.

"A.J., fill in these men on some specifics," the president said.

"Very well," Rogers said. "For the record, both of you will be court-martialed and sternly disciplined for your behavior while in the military. You will, however, be given honorable discharges. That's what the computers will show. In reality, you will have all charges against you dropped and your official record will be cleared of any wrongdoing. You will remain active military. There will be only four people besides yourselves who know of our arrangement."

"Who are they?" Marc asked.

"The president, Agent Harrison, a special liaison, and me," General Rogers replied.

"Who is the liaison?" Carl asked.

"An FBI agent," the president said. "You'll see him when we go back to the Jeep, if you agree to our offer."

"Why us? Why not the FBI or the CIA or something?" Carl asked.

"Too much red tape and too many rules. Our system of justice and our government, as wonderful as it is, puts the handcuffs on the wrong wrists. We need to fight fire with fire on the bad guy's own ground," the president said.

"The news media would chew you up and spit you out for something like this, Mr. President," Marc said.

"The media would chew me up and spit me out if they could photograph me with these shotgun shells in my coat. That's why we're up here in the mountains."

"What's to keep us from agreeing to your offer and simply disappearing?" Carl asked.

"That's not the kind of cloth either of you were cut from, Carl. You know it and so do I," the president replied.

"I still have Leeco to think about . . . and my father," Marc said.

"We will handle that for you," the president said.

"Handle it? Leeco is in ruins and my father is in a coma. How can you handle that?"

"Trust me, Marc."

Marc read the sincerity on the president's face. "I recall another president saying something like that. I never did trust him."

"Marc, you've known me personally for some time now. Have I ever lied to you?" the president asked.

"No," Marc replied.

"Then there is no need to start now, is there?"

"I suppose not."

"I will have my people provide a team of experts to take care of Leeco until your father is able to return. Leeco will also serve as your cover. When you're not on an assignment, get out on the open road and stop some of the victimization of innocent people. Essentially what I'm saying, gentlemen, is help me clean up this country."

"Meaning?" Marc asked.

"Meaning that you go after crime anywhere you can find it. Start with the trucking industry, drug operations, extortion, anything harmful and illegal. I don't think you'll have to look too far to find it. You'll be a two-man, top-secret presidential task force. I will see that you are provided with anything you need to get the job done."

"Anything?" Marc asked with a smile.

"Absolutely anything," the president said emphatically. "Anything at all."

"What you just said covers a lot of ground, Mr. President," Carl said. "Technology costs a lot of money."

"I am very aware of that, Captain Browne," the president replied. "The rampage of criminal activity in this country costs enough to clear the national debt in just a few years. American taxpaying citizens have had enough. Unfortunately, the system places a great many restraints on how far we can go to battle the criminal element. We're plagued with power-hungry lawyers and rating-starved news media. Between the two of them, this country is being devoured while the perpetrators of serious crimes laugh in our faces. And quite frankly, I'm damn tired of it."

"With all due respect, Mr. President," Marc said, "what you've just said circumvents all reasonable forms of due process of law. Isn't that what this country is all about?"

"Did you consider due process when you went after the men who killed your mother and took your father from you?"

"It was my own kind of due process," Marc said. "It was the kind those people deserved."

"Exactly. And while I would never say this or even think it in public, sometimes due process is best served from the business end of a gun. Sometimes it's the only language the criminal residue in this country understands."

"What happens if we don't accept your proposition?" Carl asked.

"Captain, I can answer that." Rogers said. "It would be an exceptional error in moral judgment for both of you. We are offering you the proverbial situation of having your cake and eating it too. You can go free with no lingering legal strings and you can both do what you're best at."

"Sir," Marc said, "we're soldiers, not cops."

The president said, "You and Carl have exhibited an exceptional attribute few men have. You both have a burning distinction between right and wrong. You also have the knowledge and ability to do something about the wrong. That combination is what this country needs. What do you say—are you in?"

"Mr. President, can the captain and I have a few minutes to discuss this alone?" Marc asked.

"I see no harm in that. Do you, General?"

"No. Go ahead, take a few minutes. Oh, and just in case you're feeling lucky, there are six snipers with Sako three-oh-eight Norma Magnum sniper rifles positioned around in the forest perimeter. So if you're feeling lucky—don't."

"Why am I not surprised?" Carl asked as he and Marc walked away from the president and General Rogers.

"Well, Captain, what do you think?" Marc asked.

"I think the jaws of democracy are clamping shut on our asses," Carl replied.

"I couldn't have said it better myself." Marc leaned over to the ground and plucked a strand of dead sage grass. He held it between his fingers and started snapping it off piece by piece until there was but a twig remaining. He stuck the twig between his teeth and started chewing on it. "You know, Carl, it might be fun. Think about it."

"Damn, man, you call dying fun? Shit, what's wrong with you?"

"They're going to throw the book at us if we tell them no. Besides, who says we're going to die? Face it, either we must know what we're doing or we're two of the luckiest bastards on the face of the earth. Right?"

"We can escape. You heard what the president said. They got nowhere to keep us if we don't want to stay."

"Maybe, maybe not. That would be a hell of a gamble."

"Yeah, you're right. Maybe we could deal with them."

"Right. How do you deal when the only other people sitting at the table have straight flushes and all you're holding is a pair of deuces? It's their game. I say we play."

"Okay, let's play. Let's take the man at his word and be damned sure we have the toys necessary to play the game right. He said we could have anything we needed. Let's start making a shopping list," Carl's face flushed with a sudden burst of excitement.

"A shopping list it is. Let's tell the man we work for him," Marc said.

"Let's," Carl said, and a broad smile exposed his white teeth.

Carl and Marc rejoined the president and General Rogers, who were strolling in the open field.

"Mr. President," Marc said, "you're the boss. When do we start?"

"Your country and I appreciate your decision. I don't think you'll regret it. And you start right now." The president smiled as he offered his handshake to Marc and Carl and they both accepted.

"Right now?" Marc asked.

"Yes, right now. You see, we have a potentially major crisis on our hands in California," the president said as his face became serious again.

"California?" Carl asked.

"Three days ago a shipment of highly toxic and potentially deadly nuclear waste was hijacked from a tractor-trailer hauling it to a secret government dump site in Northern California. The driver was killed at the scene and there were no witnesses—at least none who have come forward with information. The FBI has been involved in the case since a few hours after it happened. The powers that be at the Nuclear Regulatory Commission are having a complete shit fit, for lack of a better term."

"Who would want nuclear waste?" Marc asked as he digested what the president said.

"We don't know if they are terrorists, crackpots, or just sick fools. Whatever they are, they're playing a very deadly game. If they're bluffing, maybe we can buy enough time to find them and deal with them. If they're not, a lot of people just might die." The president put his hands into his coat pockets and flexed his shoulders.

"You indicate there has been some sort of contact with them. Has there?" Carl asked.

"Yes, yesterday. An anonymous telephone call was received by the regional office of the Environmental Protection Agency. The call was prerecorded and digitally distorted to disguise the caller's voice. All we know is it was a male caller."

"What did the tape say?" Marc asked.

"The caller demanded that fifty million dollars be wire-transferred by the United States government into three bank accounts to be designated later. He said the banks would be in London, Tokyo, and Zurich. He also demanded that I make a worldwide public apology to the People's Republic of North Vietnam for war crimes committed by our country during the Vietnam conflict," the president said.

"Damn. Are you serious?" Carl asked.

"Regretfully, I am."

"And if the government doesn't comply?" Marc asked.

"That's the bad part," the president said. "We have been given until next Wednesday to wire the money. The apology must be publicized and aired by Friday of next week. If we don't comply, he threatened to release nuclear waste into the water supplies of San Diego, Los Angeles, and Fresno. He also said three trucks would be loaded with leaking canisters of the waste material and the rigs would be driven across the United States and through major cities. The nuclear contaminants would be released into the atmosphere, leaving a trail of death and sickness all across America."

"What does the news media know about this?" Marc asked.

"Nothing yet. We've managed to keep a tight lid on it so far," Rogers said. "But that could change at any time."

"We are supposed to receive a telephone call at four o'clock today giving us bank account numbers. We have until six tomorrow evening to transfer five million in good-faith money. The caller said if we fail to do that, the next call would go to the news media and one truck would start to roll," the president said.

"If word of this gets out, our national integrity could be jeopardized," Rogers added. "There could be serious public panic and an absolute field day for the news media. It would be a crucifixion of our governmental structures."

"Marc, Carl, I want you to find the people responsible for this atrocity and deal with them as the circumstances dictate," the president said. "Get that waste product back in the hands of the NRC at all costs before innocent people start dying."

"Men," said Rogers, "I have a complete file of the scenario as it has developed. We can review it on the way back to Washington. We'll go into Fort Myers and you can select the instruments you feel you might need for this project."

"Let's go back to the Jeep and I'll introduce you to your permanent FBI liaison," the president said. "I think you'll be pleased."

The four men walked back to the black Jeep Cherokee that still sat idling in the middle of the field. The president walked to the rear door and opened it. A huge man stepped from the vehicle and stood beside General Rogers and the president. Young and muscular, his size made him look more like a linebacker than an FBI agent. Marc Lee's mouth fell open when he saw the man.

"Marc, I'd like you to meet your liaison to the federal government. This is FBI Special Agent Brittin Crain," the president said.

"Brittin?" Marc asked, stunned. "He's a Dallas cop. What liaison?"

"Good to see you, too, Marc," Crain said in his deep Texas drawl. "And Carl, you're looking good."

"*Colonel* Lee and *Major* Browne," the president said, "I'm looking forward to a long and successful relationship. Welcome aboard, men."

CHAPTER THREE

Jill Lanier sat beside Marcus Lee's bed in the ultra-high-security witness-protection safe-room in Dallas. She thumbed through a magazine, her blond hair tied back in a ponytail and her captivating blue eyes looking somewhere beyond the bound pages on her lap. Her attention was not really on the pages in front of her, but on thoughts of Marc Lee and his father. It had been well over a week since she had heard from Marc, and the Dallas police guards inside the underground concrete safe-room, although friendly enough, were little help in easing her mind. She knew something was amiss; the mysterious dreams that had taken the rest from her sleep had told her that much. Still, she wasn't exactly sure what it was. Lately, there had been no more dreams, no more subconscious link with the man she loved more than life itself.

Jill closed the magazine and laid it on the nightstand beside the bed. She took a deep breath, stretched, and then sighed. She looked at Marcus Lee. Aside from the maze of electronic gadgetry connected to him and the IV drips seeping life-giving fluids into his veins, Marc's father appeared to be simply sleeping. And in a way, that's what he was doing—sleeping. But this sleep was indefinite, induced by Bruno Segalini at the beginning of a bloody and horrible personal war between the heinous factions of organized crime and Leeco Freight Lines. It was a war

Marc and Carl had stepped forward to end almost as quickly as it had started. But then, Marc Lee and Carl Browne were experts at ending conflicts. This one, however, had involved great personal loss and sacrifice. Jill wondered what tomorrow would be like . . . if there would be a tomorrow. She wondered what life at Leeco Freight Lines would be like . . . if Leeco survived.

The thoughts etched across her mind like lightning bolts in a midsummer night sky. She thought of the two horribly evil men who had come to Leeco the first time . . . of J. T. Boswell's bloody arm thrown aimlessly on her office floor. She remembered the phone call when she learned the mob had taken Carl captive and Marc's unsheathed vengeance in rescuing his best friend. And when the mob killed Marc's mother and uncle, he expediently returned the force in like kind by destroying the Segalini compound on Long Island and killing drug kingpin Rafaello Segalini.

It all seemed so long ago, yet Jill realized it hadn't been that long at all. She recalled her own near-miss with the Grim Reaper. And once more, Marc had unleashed his cleansing sword on the forces of evil in a manner few survivors knew about. But despite the hard, forceful side of the man brought to the surface by intruding evil, he was a kind and gentle man on the inside. He was also a tender, caring, and wonderful lover. More importantly, he was her best friend again for the first time since their high school romance.

Jill focused on Marcus Lee. The giant Texas business-man's life would never be the same even if he awoke from the sleep. Everything in his world had changed, and none of it was for the better. His wife was dead, his business was destroyed, and his son had disappeared. It had been several days since Marcus had uttered words, an event Jill thought signaled his awakening. But the attending nurse had been right and Jill had been wrong; Marcus had not ascended from the darkness. But as long as his heart continued beating and his lungs drew air, there was hope. And across the vast sea of hope there was another side filled with the treasures of life waiting to be captured and lived. Marcus Lee was the kind of man who could pick up the pieces of his life from the shambled ruins and rebuild his empire out of nothing more than sheer determination. In giving life to his son, he had genetically passed along that high-energy determination.

"Miss Lanier, you have a telephone call," a police guard said.

The voice from the doorway of Marcus's room snapped her back into the present. "For me?"

"Yes. You can take the call in your bedroom if you'd like some privacy."

"Thank you," Jill replied as she stood from her chair. She crossed through the living room into her bedroom, then sat on the bed and lifted the telephone receiver from its cradle on the nightstand.

"Hello," she said.

"Hi, girl. Are you okay?"

"Marc!" she screamed. "Damn you, Marc Lee. Why haven't you called? I've been out of my mind worrying about you. Are you and Carl all right?"

"Yes, we're okay. How about you? Are you feeling better?"

"I'm great. Really, I am. The doctor said I could go home whenever I'm ready, but they won't let me out of here until Brittin gives them authorization."

"I know, that's my fault. Brittin is just doing what I asked him to do," Marc said. "How's my father?"

"He came back for a moment a week or so ago. He called me Helen and then he went back into the sleep. I think he hears what we're saying. He'll come out of it, Marc."

"Yes, I know he will. He's a very strong man."

"Just like his son. Where are you?"

"Washington, D.C."

"What's going on? I mean, I had these dreams several days ago and people were shooting at you and Carl. You were in a narrow and dark place and you couldn't get out. There was an explosion with a big ball of fire and both of you disappeared. What's happening? Am I going crazy?"

"No, you're not going crazy. As a matter of fact, it's a little spooky. You just summed up our problem near Gatlinburg, Tennessee. We're both fine now. Stop worrying and start packing."

"Packing? Am I going somewhere?"

"Well, Brittin has a new job. He's coming to Dallas to get you tomorrow."

"For what?"

"Let's call it an employment opportunity."

"What are you saying?" Jill asked. Her mind raced now and she was confused. Suddenly the conversation didn't make any sense.

"I'm saying you're about to enter an educational process that will change your entire perspective on life."

"What kind of educational process? What do you mean?"

"Carl and I are taking on a new line of work. We'll need some help from time to time. We've gotten you enrolled in the next training program for United States Marshals."

"What? But Marc, I—"

"I know, isn't it exciting?" Marc interrupted. "Just trust me, you'll love it and I bet you never regret it."

"Marc, that's just not my cup of tea."

"Sorry, I've got to go. We'll talk tomorrow when you get into Washington," Marc said as he interrupted her again.

"Washington, D.C.?"

"Bye, see you tomorrow. I love you and I can't wait to see your blue eyes."

———

Jim Yasunari was accustomed to bureaucratic red tape, but he wasn't accustomed to FBI agents roaming around his office of the Environmental Protection Agency in Los Angeles. Yasunari was a tall, lanky man in his mid-forties who took his job as head of the L.A. EPA office very seriously. On the outside, his short black hair and distinctly Japanese features didn't form an accurate composite of the man contained beneath the surface. He knew firsthand the devastating effects of nuclear energy unsheathed. It was that firsthand knowledge that had caused Yasunari to become a longtime opponent of the unsecured transportation of nuclear materials across the highways of America.

According to his application for employment at the EPA, Yasunari came to the United States when he was nine years old. As a child in Japan, he had seen the devastation, sickness, and heartbreak of atomic fission used aggressively for military purposes. His grandparents had been victims of radiation sickness from the devastating atomic attack on Hiroshima near the end of the Second World War. Even from his youth, Yasunari possessed a sharp and skillful mind. When his family relocated in Southern California, he immediately started adjusting to the American way of life. He graduated from high school with honors and attended the University of California at Los Angeles. He again graduated with honors, procuring a double major in chemistry and biology.

When Yasunari joined the EPA in 1975, he became very outspoken on matters of nuclear safety. He felt the laws of the land were all too lax where they pertained to transportation of hazardous materials. He contended that it was not a matter of *if* a major mishap would occur with a hazardous element, but rather *when* the accident would occur. His staunch stand on many crucial environmental issues had made him a number of public enemies, and at the same time gained him valuable allies within the EPA. His star rose quickly and steadily until he became director of the regional L.A. office.

Yasunari had gained the reputation within the EPA as a man whose steadfast beliefs were nonnegotiable and whose judgment was unquestionably accurate. It seemed an ironic twist that a man who so adamantly opposed overroad transportation of hazardous nuclear materials would be caught as the middleman between terrorists and the federal government.

Yasunari had taken the hot-seat position in stride and assessed the corona effects the negotiations could add to his rising bureaucratic star. He also envisioned the stolen nuclear material and the terrorist threats to be a politically catapulted grapeshot with sufficient ballistics to bring the National Transportation Safety Board to its knees. He felt that now, surely, the NTSB would see the error of its ways and make sweeping concessions regarding trucking regulations and hazardous nuclear materials.

For now, Yasunari was determined to use his present hot seat as a springboard. He could at last accomplish a dream he had sought after for as long as he could remember. And after all, what he sought would be for the benefit of the nation. If he should also benefit, then so much the better. Two birds could, indeed, be felled with the same stone.

"Mr. Yasunari it's five minutes before four. If our boy is on time, his call should come at any time. We're ready whenever he is. But remember, keep the clown on the line as long as possible so our equipment will have enough time to complete the trace," FBI Agent Benjamin Stacy said.

Stacy was a clean-cut young man who had been on his

best behavior since he and his team of communications specialists descended upon the EPA office. It was, however, an open secret that there was no love lost between the FBI and the EPA—or the FBI and any other governmental enforcement arm, for that matter. Stacy's personal attitude was that the EPA was comprised of a bunch of overly educated preppies whose goal in life was to stick their noses into other people's business.

"If the call comes, Mr. Stacy, I'm ready," Yasunari said. "I will do my best to keep the caller on the line as long as possible." He looked at his wristwatch nervously. His facial muscles tightened and he tried to hide his anxiety.

Yasunari realized the importance of handling the terrorist's call properly. It would only take one mistake, one slip of the tongue, and the results could be tragic. But on the other hand, if he handled the call as he knew he was capable, the results would be highly profitable for his future.

The FBI had moved agents into the Los Angeles area in droves since the first telephone demands were received by the EPA office. In a strategically calculated maneuver, the city of Los Angeles and the surrounding area had been gridded off on maps. FBI agents were assigned grids and the areas were under constant surveillance. Over a hundred and fifty agents were linked by F1, the FBI mobile radio service's national calling frequency. In theory, an agent could respond to any section of L.A. within forty-five seconds of being dispatched. The electronically linked web would make it difficult for a fugitive to escape the dragnet once his position had been detected. All Benjamin Stacy had to do was secure an effective trace and isolate the proper grid. At that point, the FBI would converge on the perpetrator and effect the arrest.

"Do you really think you can apprehend this caller, Mr. Stacy?" Yasunari asked.

"You just keep him on the line for thirty seconds and his ass will be mine," Stacy replied.

"I admire your confidence, Mr. Stacy. I like to see people believe in themselves."

"Thank you. I'm just doing a job I love to do. And I do it well."

"Yes, I'm quite sure you do," Yasunari said.

The intercom buzzed on Yasunari's desk. A woman's voice spoke. "A call for you on line three, Mr. Yasunari. I think it's him."

"Thank you, Karen," Yasunari said. He looked at Stacy and the electronics console in front of him. "Are you ready?"

"All units, this is Earshot One. Stand by for closing instructions," Stacy said into the speaker-microphone of the Motorola hand-held radio.

"When I say three, pick up. Ready, one, two, three . . ."

Both men picked up the telephone receivers at the exact same time.

"This is Mr. Yasunari."

"I don't really give a shit who you are, as long as you're the big dick around there. Now listen to me carefully because I'll only say this once. Five million American dollars must be transferred into account number oh-three-two-five-five-two at the Bank of Zurich within forty-eight hours. This, of course, is only a token gesture by the American government to show their intent of doing business. No gesture, and the truck rolls and good American citizens die. America will see what radiation sickness does to the human body."

"Listen to me," Yasunari said. "I don't know if the money can be moved that quickly."

"Bullshit. You know it can. The government can do anything it wants."

"No, listen. It is not my decision to make. I will have to report to my superiors. There are channels that must be followed."

"Screw your channels. The money moves in forty-eight hours or we start lighting people up like fireflies. After that, we won't be so easy to deal with."

Ben Stacy switched off the microphone on his telephone handset. He grabbed the Motorola hand-held and spoke quickly. "Grid EE-nineteen, move in. It's a pay telephone at Lincoln Boulevard and Pacific Coast Highway. All units, converge for backup."

"I must have time," Yasunari said.

"You've had your time, capitalist swine. Generations of it," the caller said. "Put up or I may even drive the truck myself. Good day." The telephone line went clear.

The radio beside the electronics console crackled with an excited voice. "One-ninety-one to Earshot. I have the suspect in sight at the telephone booth. Moving in now. Send backup!"

———

"Major Browne, did you really stick a gun barrel up some mafia henchman's ass and blow him away when you were down in Dallas?" General Rogers asked as he, Marc, and Carl walked through the polished halls of the Pentagon in Washington, D.C.

"He deserved it. The little weasel wouldn't talk, and after what they had done to Marc's father . . . well . . ."

"Don't give him such a hard time, General," Marc said. "The poor guy learned how to deal with terrorists in Delta Force."

"Some things we don't teach in antiterrorist training. Have I missed that session, or was your technique necessary field improvisation, Major?"

"Force with force—isn't that what it's all about?" Carl

said. He still wasn't quite used to being called a major. He knew it would take some time to adjust to the rank and title—but given time, he knew it would eventually sink in.

"Any word from California?" Marc asked.

"We're expecting something at any minute. You think you guys can handle it?" General Rogers asked.

"Just point us in the right direction and close your eyes," Carl replied.

"Tell me something, General. Just who came up with this project for the president?" Marc asked, changing the subject.

"He did. It's something he has wanted to do for quite some time. He wasn't sure where he would find the people. I guess your little escapade across the country showed him something."

"Why the arrest?" Carl wondered aloud.

"Effect, I suppose. I want you both to know that none of this was my idea. Once I was briefed by the president himself—well, I had to agree with him. You men are the best in the business, and that's what he needs. I support him all the way."

"What kind of egg is Harrison?" Carl asked.

"Hard boiled and dedicated. If your ass is ever in a scrape, he's your man. He plays by the book as long as it serves his purposes. If it doesn't, he tosses it out the window and fakes it."

"He comes off rock-hard, like he has no mercy or sympathy for anyone," Carl said.

"Maybe he *is* that way, I don't know. His record is impeccable and the president places his utmost trust in the man. If the big boss trusts him, so do I."

"Do you think these creeps in California have the balls to run the nuclear waste cross-country and contaminate everything?"

"Hopefully, when you men get to California tomorrow we'll never have to find out," Rogers said confidently.

"When can we start designs for the rig and supplementary equipment?" Marc asked as the men continued to walk through the corridors toward a secure elevator that would take them into Delta Force command in the underground facility far below ground level.

"It's my guess you already have," Rogers replied as they reached the elevator. He removed a magnetically encoded card key from his wallet and inserted it into the magnetic card reader. A narrow wall panel slid forward at eye level and a prerecorded computerized message instructed him to look into the lenses revealed behind the sliding panel. Rogers complied and the computer verified his individual eye structure before the elevator door opened.

"Was the president serious when he said we could have *anything* we want for this project?" A wide smile split Carl's face.

"If the boss said you could have anything you want, trust me, you'll have anything you want," Rogers replied as he encoded a sequence of numbers into the digital control of the elevator. The door closed and the elevator compartment started down.

"I'll have a bank of frequencies ready for you before we leave for California," Marc said eagerly. "I think Communications Satellite-Defense will serve our purposes nicely. We have several spare transponder uplinks available on ComSat-D and we can hit it from anywhere in the United States and most foreign countries. When I designed it that way, I really didn't have this type of project in mind." ComSat-D had been Marc's baby from electronic chip to rocket ship and finally to the stationary Earth orbit it followed twenty-five thousand miles into outer space.

"Well," Rogers said, "the boss said he would have

everything built, tested, and ready to roll within seven days from the time you tell him what you want."

Carl broke into a smile of disbelief. "Damned if I can see how he'll get it done. Reckon maybe he doesn't understand what we mean when we say *versatile overroad rig*, Marc?"

"I'm sure there will be a few surprises when we hand in the specifications. You see, General, what Carl and I have in mind isn't exactly the stereotype freight-hauling tractor and trailer. When we say versatile, we mean versatile."

"Tell the man what you want. He'll deliver," the general promised.

"I love it!" Carl clapped his hands together.

The elevator stopped and the doors opened. Agent Harrison was awaiting them. "We got the call and a rapid trace was successful. We have agents moving in as we speak. The caller has been spotted inside a telephone booth on the Pacific Coast. He should be in custody in minutes."

"Huh?" Marc mumbled. "Why does that sound too simple?" Even as he spoke the words, Marc could see the frost building on Harrison's cold face and knew he had said the wrong thing.

"I beg to differ with you, Colonel Lee. The FBI is diligently trained to do extremely good work in this type of case. We, too, are experts at dealing with terrorists. Delta Force doesn't have an exclusive on that sort of thing."

"Yes, I know," Marc said apologetically as he, Carl, and General Rogers stepped from the elevator into the control center for Delta Force. "I've seen the quality of the bureau's work before."

CHAPTER FOUR

FBI Agent Harry Hodges was the second agent to arrive in the vicinity of the pay telephone at Lincoln and Pacific Coast. He slid his unmarked car broadside through the intersection against a red traffic control light. He heard the airhorn and the screeching of tires. When he was halfway through the intersection, he narrowly missed an eighteen-wheeler that had entered on a green light. He looked up just in time to see the startled face of the Asian truck driver as he slid past the rig. He caught only a glimpse of the name on the side of the trailer. SHIMEI'S SEAFOOD IMPORTS. Although it was only a glimpse, he made a mental record of the company because he knew he would catch hell if the driver reported his license tag number.

Agent Hodges straightened the car and slid to a stop beside the other FBI car already on the scene. He saw an agent wrestling with a man at the entrance of the booth, and jumping from his car, he ran to assist.

When Hodges got closer, he realized the agent wasn't wrestling with the man at all; he was administering cardio-pulmonary resuscitation. Hodges immediately recognized the agent straddling the man on the ground as Daniel Martin.

"What the hell happened, Danny?" he asked as he knelt beside the men.

"Shit, man, we blew it," Martin said as he continued the CPR.

"What do you mean? What happened?"

"This was the phone, all right. I rolled in here and saw this guy coming out of the booth. I leveled down on him with my service revolver and identified myself. The son of a bitch just stood there. I told him to lay down on the ground and spread-eagle. That's when he collapsed. He's suffered a heart attack."

"What are you saying? Is this our man?"

"Shit no, he still had change in his hand. He's unarmed and his I.D. says he's a banker from Arkansas."

"Where's our boy, then?" Hodges asked.

"Take a look inside. These people know what they're doing. This poor bastard was just trying to figure out how to use the telephone and then I scared him to death."

"No shit. Damn, we might lose our nuts over this one," Hodges said nervously.

"Don't remind me. Go inside, you'll be fascinated." Martin worked feverishly to save the dying man on the ground.

Hodges looked inside the telephone booth as sirens approached in the distance. Hearing another siren that sounded closer, he glanced toward the street and saw the ambulance Martin had called in for the man on the ground. Hodges was careful not to disturb any evidence. He knew even a hair follicle or dandruff could be used as conclusive evidence once a suspect was apprehended. What he saw caused him to drop his jaw and shake his head in disbelief. Then he knew what Dan Martin meant . . . these people were good and they knew what they were doing.

"What do you think of that?" Martin asked.

Hodges looked up and saw the paramedics running toward the booth. "Unbelievable. Maybe the lab can find something on this mess."

"I wouldn't count on it. Anyone this smart isn't likely to screw up by leaving anything to link them here. These people aren't dummies, they're slick," Martin said.

The paramedics reached the men and immediately took over, relieving Martin. They started checking for a pulse and respiration. One paramedic, whose name tag said T. Simmons, applied a blood pressure cuff and connected a heart monitor. Another, with a tag saying C. Bell, administered CPR. The men worked for a few minutes, then looked at the two FBI agents.

"He didn't make it. This man is dead," Simmons said. "Sorry."

"This man is probably over sixty years old," Bell said. "What did he do?"

"He walked into the wrong phone booth at the wrong time," Martin said. "It was just real bad timing."

"Too bad," Hodges said. "Anyway, what do you make of this, Dan?"

Martin stood and looked into the telephone booth. "From what I can see, the slimebag wired the telephone line and then made the call. It looks like a duplex transceiver in two parts. He could talk and listen at the same time, just like a regular telephone—only difference is, he did it from somewhere else. The lab will probably tell us more, but I figure the bastard wasn't within a dozen blocks of this phone booth. He did it all by radio. He probably sat and laughed his ass off when we swarmed in here. When he'd laughed until his side hurt, the son of a bitch probably just drove away."

"Damn," Harry Hodges said. "Friggin' high technology."

"Yeah," Daniel Martin agreed. "Look at that, the whole damn thing isn't as big as a package of cigarettes."

"Have you told Stacy?"

"Not yet. I've got to get my ass ready for it first," Martin said, and he wiped the cold beads of perspiration from his forehead with his shirtsleeve.

"If it's any consolation, I'll probably be there with you when the ass-reaming starts. I almost creamed a seafood truck coming in here. Scared the shit out of the little Asian guy driving it, too," Hodges said.

"Great," Dan Martin said. "Our boy got away and I've got a dead Arkansas banker on my hands. Somehow, I don't think the director will understand."

———

Nagai Soseki stopped the eighteen-wheel rig inside the east L.A. warehouse. He closed the warehouse doors and immediately started removing the stick-on lettering from the side of the trailer. When he was finished, he placed new letters on the trailer. What had been displayed as a seafood importer's rig twenty minutes before was now Coastal Freightways of San Francisco. The fact that the rig had been stolen three days earlier in Flagstaff, Arizona, made little difference. Every conceivable number that could be traced had been removed or altered. Even the independent driver who owned the rig wouldn't recognize it now. What had been an all-white cab-over-engine International tractor was now navy-blue metallic with intricate graphics and scrolls.

Soseki was a slender, short man with jet-black hair and a black mustache. His rugged face gave him stereotypical truck driver looks with an Asian twist. He seldom smiled because he concentrated his mental power always on whatever task was at hand. His looks were a deceptive contradiction, however, because the man behind them was a highly educated man who held a doctorate degree in nuclear physics from Cal Tech. The game of terrorism was new to him, but death from radiation wasn't. Soseki, like tens of thousands of other Japanese natives, was a direct descendant of nuclear holocaust.

Soseki opened the doors on the rear of the eighteen-wheel rig and lifted a two-wheel dolly from its restraining straps inside. Rolling the dolly to three large crates in a darkened corner of the nearly empty warehouse, he lifted a corner of the first crate and slid the lip of the dolly under it. He let the crate fall back onto the two-wheel and started for the trailer.

Soseki made short work of moving all three crates. He secured the trailer, opened the warehouse door, and headed for the open road . . . for victorious recognition of a lethal menace.

He had already put the full-duplex VHF transceiver into a suitcase and stowed it away in the sleeper of the International COE rig. He thought back at the police car he had almost collided with as he left the area of the telephone booth. He would have loved to see the face of the lawman when he reached the telephone booth and found nothing there except his transceiver wired into the telephone lines. It pleased him that technology had advanced so rapidly.

Soseki turned the International onto I-5 North. Within hours, he would be transferring canisters of nuclear waste and preparing to follow through with the threats he and his accomplices had made to the government of the United States. It soothed Soseki's mind to know that in less than a week he and his friends would be fifty million dollars richer and there would be unstoppable cries from the American public for immediate regulatory legislation to ban transportation of hazardous nuclear waste. Even if the government refused to pay the money as demanded, the public would still be outraged when the word got out that lethal nuclear materials had been stolen so easily. Either way it went, Friends of Humanity would win and the descendants of nuclear destruction would make their point. Soseki knew that sometimes it was necessary to take bold steps to save civilization from itself—and frequently those steps demanded extreme sacrifices.

As Soseki drove north on I-5, he mentally reviewed the plan. He had just made the second contact with a responsible agency of the federal government. He had secured the acquisitioned radiation suits from the warehouse in east Los Angeles. Once the suits were deposited at the storage site with the stolen canisters, he and Mori Osamu could implement the second phase of the operation. He knew the Americans wouldn't continue to sit idly by and let them release nuclear materials across the continental United States. The government would have to make a move, and in doing so would make certain pertinent concessions. And try as the government agents may, there was no way they could ever find the stolen canisters before the plan was set into motion. Mori Osamu had assured him that the government would have to spend far too much time untangling bureaucratic red tape to move effectively against their plan. The government had lost, and mankind was the ultimate winner.

———

"They did what? How? Tell me how that is possible! I want explanations and answers, not excuses. I expect a full report on my desk by zero-eight-hundred tomorrow," Agent Harrison said sharply into the telephone.

Marc Lee watched in amusement as the stone-faced Fed expressed his disgust. Marc thought it interesting to see Harrison excited. He hadn't seen the man waver from hard rock since he had known him. Marc motioned General A.J. Rogers to follow him, then stood up from his chair in Rogers's office at Delta Force command in the Pentagon as Harrison continued to converse with agents in Los Angeles. General Rogers followed as they left the office.

"What's on your mind?"

"From the sound of that conversation, I'd say the FBI botched it," Marc said.

"It looks that way. Maybe now I see why the president decided to approach things from a different angle."

"We may have to move sooner than we expected. How quickly can we get the equipment I asked for?"

"A few hours at the most. What's your plan?"

"I think Carl and I need to go to California as soon as we can get a full report from Harrison."

"Okay, but try not to tread too heavily on the bureaucratic toes. There is enough animosity between agencies of the federal government. I don't think the FBI is thrilled over your project as it is," Rogers warned.

"That's Harrison's problem. If the still water runs too deep, why is the FBI involved in this project?"

"You'll have to ask the president about that one. It was his choice. Maybe he felt the time would come when there could be unity and camaraderie for the overall cause, I don't know."

"From what you've said and my past experience with the system, it appears all of the agencies have their own little exclusive domains and the pedestals are closely guarded havens. Do you think this is what George Washington and Thomas Jefferson had in mind?"

"Not likely, but things were a lot simpler then," the general replied.

"Yeah, maybe you're right. But simple or not, the basics have always remained the same. I wonder what Washington and Jefferson would say if they could see this country today?"

"They'd probably throw up."

"Probably," Marc agreed.

"General, could I see you and Colonel Lee in here for a

moment?" Agent Harrison stood in General Rogers's office doorway.

Rogers and Marc walked back into the private room and closed the door.

"We blew it," Harrison said.

"Meaning?" Marc asked.

"Our people secured the trace when the call came in at EPA Los Angeles. It was a telephone booth near the ocean in Santa Monica. Our people moved in quickly. There was an elderly man leaving the phone booth when our first agent arrived. Our agent proceeded to apprehend the man and he collapsed—had a heart attack and died."

"So your link to the stolen nuclear material died?" Rogers asked.

"Not exactly. You see, the man was vacationing in Malibu with his wife. He was a banker from Little Rock, Arkansas. His name was Calvin Price. He had nothing to do with the phone call," Harrison said sheepishly.

"I don't understand," Marc said.

"The telephone booth was wired with a transceiver. Whoever made the call did it from another position by radio. And the banker, well, he was at the wrong place at the wrong time. He had just entered the telephone booth to make a call."

"And it cost him his life," Marc added.

"Yes," Harrison said.

"Damn," General Rogers said. "What now?"

"We get to work," Marc said. "Where is the NRC in all this?"

"Pissed, but willing," Harrison said. "Why?"

"If the people responsible for the theft of this California shipment were smart enough to know when and where to hit it, they may be after more of the same thing. Is there any way to stop, at least temporarily, the movement of any other waste products?"

"Maybe, but we have to be careful," Harrison said. "Remember, the public knows nothing of this situation as of yet."

"Good, we need to keep it that way for as long as we can," Marc said.

"I don't think it's us that we need to worry about. The people who have that stuff have also threatened to place a call to a major news network and tell them everything if we don't start moving the money like they've instructed."

"Great, that's all we need. We get the media in on this and then the defecation will certainly engage the rotary oscillator," Marc said with a grin.

"What?" asked Harrison with a puzzled expression filling his face.

"The shit will hit the fan," Marc said.

"Okay, what do you suggest?" Harrison asked as he looked Marc squarely in the eyes.

"Carl and I need to move to California as quickly as we can. Since these people are intent upon driving a load of nuclear death across the country, that tells me a lot."

"Such as?"

"First, they probably aren't willing to contaminate themselves, so they must have the equipment necessary to handle the materials safely. That tells me they must also have the expertise. I don't figure they will chance death from radiation when there is still a chance they could gain fifty million dollars. Would you?"

"You're asking the wrong person, but no, I don't believe I would," Harrison replied. "But don't forget, this is probably a conspiracy with many people involved. Sacrifices would be expected."

"True. What has the bureau done so far?"

"We have scrutinized a computerized data base of every known terrorist, antigovernment, or left-wing faction in the country that has an interest in social unrest. Of course, at the head of the list are the factions that publicly criticize our nuclear policies. You know, the ones who sit in at nuclear power plants, carry placards, and generally bitch and moan through the media."

"Have you turned up anything in that direction?" Marc asked.

"Yes, but the listings are too extensive to be humanly covered in the time frame we're dealing with."

"So you're saying at best it's hit or miss."

"Simplistically put, yes," Harrison said. "We're looking at this from a couple of angles. It could be just a clear-cut case of some radical group seeking funding, but it could also be a publicity stunt to gain momentum for a political faction."

"It could also be a disgruntled trucking company pissed off because they didn't get a government contract. Don't forget that angle," Marc said.

"Not likely. But that is a new twist we hadn't considered."

"Gentlemen, the possibilities are endless. The problem is, what do we do about it now?" General Rogers asked.

"General, doesn't the Air Force have jet fighters equipped with radiation sensing devices capable of detecting abnormal levels of radiation from high altitudes?"

"Yes, what are you thinking?"

"Let's put them to work on a training mission. Put them in the air over the western United States and see what they produce."

"It's a thought. We also have satellites with ultrasensitive detection capabilities. But none of that will do any good until the canisters are opened. By then it may be too late," Rogers said.

"Maybe, maybe not. It could be a link we don't have now, if we can find an open canister."

"Do either of you have any idea how much active

radiation there is floating around out there in this country?" Harrison said. "I'm not even sure we have the manpower to trace something like that down without calling in a full-scale military operation."

"General, can you have some specialized communications equipment in place in California by tomorrow morning?" Marc asked.

"Yes, of course. What do you need?"

"I want to work off ComSat-D. We can use one of the digitally scrambled uplinks and downlink into the defense repeater system on VHF. I want Carl and me to have constant communications when we leave here."

"What are you going to put it in?" Rogers asked.

"The eighteen-wheeler you'll have waiting for us when we get to California," Marc replied.

"What eighteen-wheeler?"

"I don't know, but find us one. We don't have time to drive there. We'll need the Learjet. Oh, and toss in a spectrum analyzer just in case these people decide to toss out some more radio frequency energy," Marc said.

"Why a truck?" Harrison asked.

"Because they can't haul nuclear waste in the trunk of a car. They've got to have a truck of some sort. If we're in an eighteen-wheeler, we'll blend in without calling attention to ourselves."

"Isn't that a little slow?" Harrison asked.

"Yes, that's why we'll need a Jeep Cherokee to haul in the back of the rig. Our Ram got terminated in Gatlinburg and it was a tight fit anyway. Be sure the Cherokee is a four-door four-by-four and has at least a four-liter engine. We'll make the modifications when this is done," Marc said.

"Modifications?" Harrison asked. His face appeared puzzled for the second time in minutes.

"Later," Marc replied. "Carl is at the armory now. He

should have the weapons we might need on this mission. If we find a need for anything else, we'll call you."

"Anything else?" Harrison asked.

"Yeah, I like black Jeeps."

CHAPTER FIVE

"This nuclear waste is some pretty heavy-duty business," Carl said as he closed the file folder. He adjusted his seat belt and looked out of the small round window beside him. The Learjet was clearly twenty-five thousand feet above the ground or higher. Everything on the surface below appeared as tiny dots streaming by in a panorama of mixed colors.

"It's not my line of expertise, but I'm guessing we're both in for a heavy education. If these people pull the stopper on one of these things while we're near it, I guess we can kiss our asses good-bye," Marc said.

"Knowing what you know now, do you think we've made the right decision?" Carl said as the Learjet thrust its way through the American sky on an all-out run to California.

"Did we really have a choice?"

"The deck was stacked against us, wasn't it?"

"No shit. I'll give the president one thing—when he decided we were his people, he covered all of the bases. Legally, they had us by the balls."

"Do you think he would have let the legal authorities go through with it?"

"Does a frog bump his ass?" Marc asked with a smile.

"He sure picked a good one to start us on, didn't he?"

"Yeah. By the way, have you put much thought into the

design of the rig? You did as much or more driving than me when we were on the road. What do you think we'll need?"

"Everything we can imagine, and then some. If this nuclear shit is an indication of the kind of thing The Man has in store for us, nothing's too good."

"Maybe it will get easier after this one," Marc said.

"I'll make some more notes on the rig while we're out this time. I think it needs to be fast and have long range. The most important thing is communications and fire-power. If we've got that, we can fake the rest of it," Carl said.

"Right. We'll need satellite data links as well as voice. It should have multimode high frequency, very high fre-quency, and ultrahigh frequency capabilities. And we need enough firepower to be a two-man army. If there is any room left, we can work on creature comforts."

"Like showers, cooking facilities, sleeping arrange-ments, that kind of thing?"

"Exactly. Let's not forget totally independent power plants with long-term backup facilities," Marc added.

"How about armor?"

"Harrison said they would contract the same people who did the presidential limousines. They're the best there is. Hey, did you know there are a lot of high-tech advance-ments in lightweight mobile armor?"

"No. Like what?"

"Kevlar, for one thing. We can put that to good use. And some of the metal alloys used in the manned space projects . . . wow!" Marc said.

"This could be fun if we make it back from California," Carl said, laughing.

"Right, you're the eternal optimist. Seriously, one of the most important elements in building this rig is cosmetics. The overall package has to be exactly like every other eighteen-wheeler on the highway, from the outside. Even a discriminating eye shouldn't be able to detect any difference."

"That's what we black folk been saying for years. It's what's inside that counts," Carl said.

"I want to be able to live in the rig and work out of it for long periods of time without have to restock. I want it to do everything but drive itself and forecast the weather."

"You know, that last part may not be a bad idea. It never hurts to know in advance when a storm is brewing," Carl concluded.

"Speaking of storms, why don't you get Delta Control on the horn and let's see if the general has gotten those satellite pictures I asked for."

"Yes sir, Colonel. Damn, Marc, I can't get used to calling you a colonel. Why'd he do that, anyway?"

"Because he likes our faces. Now call the man."

Carl lifted the intercom handset to the cockpit of the Learjet. The copilot answered in seconds. "Would you get me a clear line to Delta Control, please."

"Yes, sir," replied John Atkinson, the copilot. "It may take a minute or two. Is it urgent?"

"No, not urgent, but top priority," Carl said.

"Very well. Stand by," Atkinson said.

"He's getting us a line. It may be a minute or two." Carl looked at Marc. "What's your idea on those satellite photos, anyway?"

"I have a plan. If we can find something with reasonable definition, I think we can trace the stolen waste shipment in short order."

"How so?"

"Depending upon the exact time the hijacking took place, we might get a photograph of the culprits out on the highway."

"How?"

"The National Oceanographic and Atmospheric Administration takes satellite photos constantly. Sometimes the resolution is incredible, sometimes it isn't. Narrowing down the time would give us a starting place to work into their file photos of last Monday. I'm betting the stolen goods didn't go too far. The rig that was transporting the materials hasn't been recovered. My money says the canisters are still on the truck."

"But the rig could be anywhere," Carl said. "California is a hell of a big place—and that's assuming this stuff is still in the state."

"You're aware of the pinpoint accuracy we've built into our wrist transponders, right?"

"Sure, they've saved my butt a time or two."

"We can do the same thing with infrared photographs from outer space. If these guys open the canisters, we can pinpoint them even if they're in a cave somewhere. The Russians have been doing it for years with their orbiting spacecraft."

"I still don't think I fully understand," Carl said.

"We need a link . . . someplace to start. I think the satellite photos will give us that."

"What if it was cloudy in that part of California last Monday?"

"NOAA isn't the only one with a satellite we can access. There are other avenues and some of them are of even better quality than NOAA."

"I'll take your word for it," Carl said. "You know, I'm sure as hell glad I'm on your side. You'd make a real bad enemy."

"Don't give me too much credit. I'm ninety-nine percent nice guy and only one percent mean, hateful, and vindictive. I just like to get the job done," Marc said with a broad smile.

"So I've noticed. This is one job I'll be glad to put a cap

on. All this nuclear shit gives me the creeps. I'm ready to hit the road and drive an eighteen-wheeler."

"Give it time, my friend. Just give it time. You'll get all of the road you can handle. After all, this is just the beginning."

"I'm ready to roll out on the highways," Carl said. "With all this nuclear crap . . . shit. Face it, I ain't into glowing in the dark. You know what I mean?"

"Look at it this way," Marc said. "Everything has changed in our lives in the past few weeks and it's still changing. We can never go back and nothing will ever be the same as it was before we left Fort Bragg on leave. It's all past—all of it. Until we get the kinks ironed out of the president's pet project, we're caught in the middle of the transition."

———

Brittin Crain relaxed on the long flight from Washington, D.C., to Dallas. It gave him time to digest and then absorb the great changes that had entered his life in the past week. And the more he concentrated on what had happened to him since the FBI had arrested him in Dallas and his meeting with Marc, Carl, and the president of the United States in the forests of Virginia, the more he admired the man elected to lead the country. The president had been quite thorough in his approach for establishing a top-secret crime-fighting task force. Personally, Crain felt there were no better men for the job than Marc Lee and Carl Browne.

Crain and Marc had been high school classmates and best friends. The friendship had endured through the years, even while Marc was on active duty with Delta Force. And while his friend had been flying all over the world in pursuit of justice and protection for innocents, Brittin had evolved into a top-notch street cop. Dallas had been his world and the criminal scum had been his target. He, like Marc, had sailed through the ranks and held the rank of lieutenant prior to the FBI's intervention. In many respects, the friends were just alike—two hard-boiled Texans fighting for what they believed in. And when they believed in something, they fought hard with a fury that knew no boundaries.

It was that fury that had landed Crain in the position he now held: FBI agent, for the records; liaison, for the purpose. He had been skeptical when he was approached with the idea of working for the federal government. At first, he didn't trust the men from Justice because their methodology had been more than slightly coercive. But being a realist, it took little conversation to change his way of thinking. The FBI agents who questioned him emphasized the many violations of law he had committed in his association with Marc and Carl. In essence, the hardened jaws of the Justice Department had his testicles in their saber-toothed grip, and that simplified Crain's choices drastically. What the gleaming Gold Shields didn't know was that he would have gladly traded one of his testicles for the job, anyway. So by reciprocal consent, Crain and the president of the United States got what they each wanted.

It was all like a dream to Crain. The rapid change from a Dallas police lieutenant to a presidential liaison on top-secret status wasn't without cost. The Feds covered their tracks well. Crain's superiors at the Dallas Police Department were notified that Crain was being questioned for his association with Marc and Carl. Two days after his questioning started, they received his formal resignation from the department. In a show of true public relations mastery, the police department managed to cover Crain's involvement with federal fugitives and keep the story from the media. Brittin Crain simply walked away and the face of the Dallas Police Department was left unscarred. It was a clean cut, and Crain's new position of high authority was never exposed. The loose ends were all tied down . . . all except Jill Lanier.

Jill's link to Marc and Crain extended back to their high school days. It was a base that had to be covered and the president had formulated plans to cover it. When Marc and Carl agreed with the president's proposal, a conversation ensued that would forever change Jill Lanier from a blue-eyed blond secretary to a woman secure in her personal abilities. The petite young woman was about to learn the arts of survival and honed instinct. Crain had been given his first assignment: Convince Jill Lanier she needed the training. In a few days, she would go from punching keys on a typewriter to punching holes in paper targets. Her level of proficiency would increase until she was an astute contributing support member of the president's top-secret team. And only when she had mastered her assignment would she be told why it was all necessary.

The flight was flawless, but Crain was glad to be on the ground again. He left the 737 jetliner carrying his only luggage, a carryon overnight bag provided for him by a Justice Department expense account. He made his way through the maze at Dallas–Fort Worth International Airport and rented a car on the same expense account. As he signed the credit card receipt, he realized he was starting to like the federal way of doing things. It was straight and to the point—get the job done. The president had personally authorized unlimited expenditures for the project. It was carte blanche with only one requirement, and that being the criminals had to go down—permanently.

The drive to the underground safe-room took forty-five minutes. Crain parked the car and entered the building through his usual entrance, then took the elevator to the third basement subfloor. At the access door he encoded a numerical string and waited for the door lock to buzz, signaling an alarm shutdown and authorized entry. He opened the first steel security door and stepped to the intercom inside the alcove preceding another high-security door. There he pressed the intercom button and waited.

"Entry code, please," the voice said over the intercom speaker.

"Poppycock," Crain replied.

"That you, Lieutenant?" asked the voice.

"In person, Alvarez. Let me in. I've come for Jill."

"Okay, Lieutenant, enter your end of the code and I'll follow." Detective Juan Alvarez was surprised to hear from Crain without receiving an advance telephone call. He knew the big cop had been conspicuously absent for several days. He had also listened to Jill complain that she hadn't heard from anyone since she was left in the safe-room. When the call had come from Marc Lee the day before, Alvarez was almost relieved that the girl would be leaving soon. But even so, Alvarez had decided to play the next move the safe way.

"Let it rip," Crain said.

It was almost instantly that a green LED appeared on the digital keypad beside the door. Crain punched in a second series of numbers and waited for the door to open.

"Nice to see you, Lieutenant." Alvarez lowered the M-16 automatic rifle he had pointed at Crain's head when the door swung open. He stepped from behind a concrete barrier built inside the entry room specifically for doorway security.

"Yes," Crain replied. "It's good to see you're still so proficient at your job. For a second there, I thought maybe you were going to shoot me."

"Just using caution, Lieutenant. No personal offense intended." Alvarez was small with pitch-black hair that was balding on the top. He had dark skin and a lean face that was well weathered. Even to an untrained observer, the man holding the M-16 certainly looked as if he would use it with little provocation.

"None taken. Where's Jill?"

"Sleeping. You want me to wake her up?"

"No, let me do it. The surprise will do her good," said Crain.

"That bedroom over there," Alvarez said as he pointed to a room off of the living area of the apartmentlike complex.

"Thanks," Crain said as he walked to the door. He knocked and waited. When there was no reply, he entered slowly. Jill was sound asleep.

"She sleeps like she's dead," Alvarez said from the doorway.

"Seems to be a lot of that going around. Let me wake her."

"I'll be out here if you need me."

Crain turned around and faced Jill. He stepped softly to the side of her bed, leaned over, and placed his hand on her shoulder. "Jill. Jill, wake up. We've got a long trip ahead of us. You need to get ready."

Jill responded slowly at first, then she sat up in the bed. She looked at Crain through glazed, sleepy eyes. "Brittin. Oh, I'm so glad you're here. How's Marc?"

"He's all right and anxious to see you."

"When can I see him?" Jill started to get out of the bed.

"Soon. How is Marcus?"

"He's still in a coma, but his vital signs are strong."

"So nothing has changed?"

"I was hoping you would tell me. What's going on, anyway?"

"Change. Get dressed, we've got a plane to catch."

"Where are we going?"

"To start a new way of life," Crain said. "I think you're going to like it."

———

The white government Learjet taxied to a stop beside a gray metal hangar at Edwards Air Force Base. The powerful engines whined down and the cabin door opened. A man in a dark suit, white shirt, and sunglasses stood outside the cabin door. Marc Lee was the first to exit the plane and his first glance at the man told him he was a federal agent.

"Mr. Lee, I presume. I am Special Agent Gary Merrill." The man behind the sunglasses extended an open hand to Marc.

"My pleasure, Mr. Merrill," Marc said. "This is Mr. Browne." Marc turned and gestured a hand to Carl.

"My superiors in Washington speak quite highly of both of you. The Nuclear Regulatory Commission is fortunate to have men like you in their organization," Merrill said.

"Thank you," Marc said. Carl simply nodded as a sign of thanks.

"We have the equipment you requested and some additional information from Washington. We're ready whenever you are," Merrill said.

"Good," Marc said. "Let's go find this material before it's too late." He let his mind slip away for just a moment. The foundation was laid: He and Carl would be operating as investigators for the NRC. So far, Washington had done just fine.

Marc and Carl accompanied the FBI agent to the hangar. Aside from a fluorescent orange wind sock drifting with the warm California breeze, the hangar was all drab gray. Two giant sliding metal doors spanned the front of the building. A lone window just above ground level occupied one small corner near the right front of the building. As the men approached, a walk-in door beside the window opened. A man wearing Air Force blues and captain's bars stepped from the door.

"Good evening, gentlemen. I'm Captain Perry Price. I've been assigned to your project until its completion. I've also been instructed to make your stay at Edwards as pleasant as possible, so if you'll follow me, I'll go over our preliminary preparations." Price was very fit, his uniform pressed and neat. He looked to be in his late twenties. He was probably six feet tall and near 175 pounds. He had auburn hair and light, freckled skin. He was, no doubt, military through and through, but still quite pleasant.

Marc noticed the wings pinned to his chest above his shirt pocket. The auburn hair and boyish face didn't fit the deep voice projected by Price, but the wings stirred Marc's curiosity.

The men exchanged greetings and continued to walk into the hangar, following Captain Price.

"I noticed your wings, Captain. What do you fly?" Marc asked.

"My primary aircraft is an F-15 Eagle, sir," Price said.

"A nice aircraft, so I hear. And pretty quick, too." Marc was visibly impressed and his respect for the pilot skyrocketed instantly. The F-15, by any accounts, was a lean and fast military machine crammed full of sophisticated technology and weaponry. Schoolboys didn't fly it; only the best got their hands on the stick of an F-15 Eagle.

"Yes sir, it is rather quick. She'll cruise at twice the speed of sound," Price said affectionately.

"My, my, that is quick," Marc said. "You think maybe we can get this project wrapped up with the same speed?"

Price laughed. "We'll do our very best, sir."

The men entered the hangar and a small office alcove separated from the huge main interior of the metal building. A conference table sat in the middle of the office, with folding metal chairs around it. In the center lay a stack of black and white photographs filled with reference lines and numbers.

"If we could all be seated, we'll go over the information from the Washington bureau," Merrill said.

The men pulled up chairs and gathered around the table. Among the men in suits and uniforms, Marc and Carl stood out like the proverbial sore thumb. They were both dressed in denim jeans, light plaid flannel shirts, and black jump boots. But their dress was both comfortable and functional for the mission. And to Marc and Carl, that's all that mattered.

"Now," Merrill said, "I trust each of you has taken the opportunity to review the file on this case. If you haven't, I have a couple copies here. As you are all aware, we must move quickly on this matter. As an update, the bureau has transported the radio device located in a telephone booth in Santa Monica to the FBI national laboratory. We could have a full analysis at any minute. Hopefully, there will be some clue to the identity of the person or persons involved in this madness."

"Is there any possible link to the banker from Arkansas?" Carl asked.

"None so far," Merrill replied.

"Captain Price, do you have infrared-equipped aircraft here at Edwards?" Marc asked.

"Yes, we are prepared to make thèm airborne at your discretion. You'll have the full cooperation of the Air Force. You just say the word, Mr. Lee," Price said.

"After we finish reviewing these photos, Mr. Browne and I will probably head out on the highway. You do have our overroad rig, don't you?"

"It's in the hangar," Price replied. "Equipped with everything you asked for."

"Good. We'll need that to make our move."

"I have a question, Mr. Lee," Merrill said.

"Sure."

"Why would investigators from the NRC want to travel in a tractor and trailer?"

"That's simple," Carl said. "If you're trying to stalk a wolf, you have to look like one. If you're looking for a truckload of nuclear waste, you've got to come off like a trucker."

"Carl's right," Marc added. "And besides that, we like them."

"I see," Merrill said. "I was just curious."

"No problem," Marc replied. "Now, let's get to these satellite maps. I think our lost nuclear waste is somewhere on these pages. We just have to find it."

CHAPTER SIX

Nagai Soseki shrugged his shoulders and stretched. His first conscious thought upon awakening was that his nostrils burned from the stench of kerosene. He sat up in his cot and his back ached. His second conscious thought was that he wasn't as young as he used to be, and his body constantly reminded him of that fact. Sleeping all night on a cot in a dark and damp cave was difficult for a man in his fifties.

Soseki stood from the cot and looked around the cave. Dozens of other cots were filled with men still sleeping. He noticed the blackened globes of a half-dozen kerosene lanterns flickering in the darkness. Tiny trails of thin black smoke rose from each lantern, polluting the crisp cave air with the smell of kerosene and giving off a dull yellow glow. The lanterns were the only illumination inside the otherwise black crevice.

Soseki rubbed his arms with his hands to generate body heat and warm himself. He glanced to the left of the area where the men lay sleeping. The flatbed trailer appeared as it had when he had given in to sleep the night before. The canisters of nuclear waste material were still chained to the trailer. Today, Soseki knew that would all change. Today, the Friends of Humanity would cause the eyes of all civilized nations to fall upon their work. Soseki smiled to himself and then quietly walked to the mouth of the giant cave.

A young Asian man perched on a rock outcropping snapped to attention when Soseki stepped from the cave.

"Ah, good morning, Professor," the man said. "I trust you rested well."

"Thank you, Mishima Ogai. Yes, I slept as well as can be expected in such primitive conditions," Soseki replied. "Is all quiet this morning?"

"Yes, Professor. The night passed quickly and pleasantly. Perhaps it is the adrenaline rush from the very nature of our undertaking." Ogai shifted the battered .45-caliber Thompson submachine gun around on his lap.

"Yes, perhaps," Soseki replied. "Has there been any word from Mori Osamu since my telephone call to the EPA yesterday?"

"Yes, just after you retired last evening. I believe Izumi Shimada spoke with him. Izumi is now in the communications shack and he is probably still sleeping. I'm sure he would be honored to speak with you."

"I shall visit him now." Soseki stretched his arms and back muscles. "Perhaps he will have a pot of green tea simmering on the stove. I need something to stir me awake."

"Perhaps you should consider *sake*, Professor. Certainly that would awaken you," Ogai said, and his young face split in a broad smile.

"Only after my morning tea, young pilgrim. At my age, I must salvage my disgestive tract," Soseki said as he patted his stomach and smiled.

Soseki turned from the young sentry and started across the compound to a run-down old wooden building used as a communications shack. He scanned the rock pinnacles surrounding the canyonlike yard of the compound as he walked. The yard was surrounded on three sides by high, jutting rock cliffs. Ten men, all armed with salvaged automatic weapons of World War II and Korean War vintage, stood guard around the yard. The yard itself lay at the mouth of the cave and was about the size of two football fields lined side by side. It was barren ground, packed down many years ago by the sandaled feet of Japanese predecessors and military jeeps.

As Soseki continued to walk to the communications shack, he stepped from the cool shadows of the mountain peaks into the first rays of the morning sun. The sunlight sent a soothing warmth over him and caused him to shiver lightly. He glanced once more around the compound, to the rows of dilapidated barracks built against the foot of the cliffs. Once they were filled with the pleasing odor of freshly cut lumber, but now they were sad monuments to mankind's lack of basic understanding. And for a long moment, Soseki wondered what horror and endless sorrow his countrymen had known in this place before his time here. The thought caused him to shiver again, and this time it wasn't lightly.

Soseki pushed the door of the shack open. He noticed as he stepped inside that it was held in place by only one hinge. There were two others on the door frame, but they were long since rusted away. Shimada was already awake and sitting by a radio console when Soseki entered.

"Izumi, I see you have awakened early," Soseki said. "I like that."

"Yes, Professor, I am a light sleeper," Shimada replied. He was a short man and barely over twenty-one. His thin black hair was cut short and combed to the right side. He was heavier than most young Japanese men, though he fell short of being called fat. He was a brilliant student and dedicated to the purpose.

"I am told Mori Osamu contacted us last night. What information did he have to relay?"

"He said the project was proceeding nicely. Your telephone call was successful and the government agents are quite concerned."

"As well they should be. Did he offer any information about the transfer of the funds?"

"No. He did say he would contact us again before nine o'clock this morning."

"Very well. Is that green tea steeping on the stove?"

"Yes, help yourself," Shimada said, glancing to a flat-topped potbelly stove in one corner of the room.

Soseki walked to the stove, picked up an earthernware cup from a shelf beside it, and poured himself a cup of tea. Steam rose as the warm liquid met the cooler air. Soseki immediately started sipping the soothing substance.

"We must soon make our preparations to move the waste product if the government fails to deliver our good-faith money. We must not back down, or the purpose will be lost," Soseki said as he sipped gingerly at the steaming cup.

"I agree, Professor. The purpose of our project is much too important to rescind our actions now," Shimada said.

"Always remember, Izumi, what we do, we do for the sake of mankind . . . for the sake of our departed ancestors."

"I have never forgotten that, Professor. You look tired. Did you not sleep restfully?" Shimada asked.

"No, I didn't. A cave is not a comfortable place to live. But if we fail at our purpose, what remains of mankind will be committed to cave habitation for generations to come. We must make society reckon with a new level of awareness before the madness is irreversible. Wanton nuclear reck-lessness must be halted and a new way of thinking insti-tuted. It is our purpose to cause society to make that transition."

———

"I still don't understand what you're looking for on these satellite photographs," Merrill said as he, Price, Marc, and Carl scanned the photos on the table.

"A clue," Marc said.

"But from weather photos?"

"Granted, the resolution isn't great, but with enlargements we may find the truck that was hauling the nuclear waste materials."

"You're serious, aren't you?" Merrill asked.

"Very serious. Look closely," Marc said. "If you'll scan these enlargements of the area where the rig was hijacked, you'll see a finer definition of the terrain. That's our first hint."

"Sorry, Mr. Lee, but I don't understand," Merrill said.

"Get the photos from our surveillance satellites over there." Marc pointed to another stack of photos. "Now look here. You see these bright glitches in random areas around the state?"

"Yes. What do they mean?" Merrill asked.

"They are heat-activated glitches. Some abnormal level of heat caused that glitch. As you can see, they are almost a solid mass around the highly populated urban areas. Get up here in Northern California in the mountains, and they tend to dissipate drastically."

"So what does that prove?"

"In itself, nothing. These photos are from infrared-sensitive equipment. What we need to do is take two or three days of the photographs and make comparisons. I think we can find the stolen load with that," Marc said.

"Maybe I can help a little, gentlemen," Price said.

"Damn. Please do," Merrill said. "I don't know what the hell you people are talking about."

"What Mr. Lee is saying is that the United States has satellite facilities in orbit that can make computerized comparisons of surface and subsurface temperatures. The sensitivity of these birds is staggering. Some of them are sensitive enough to detect a small campfire inside a cave in the side of a mountain."

"What the hell good is that? We're not looking for campfires, we're looking for stolen nuclear waste." Merrill undid the top button on his shirt. In the same motion, he loosened his tie and moved his head back and forth two or three times to relieve his tension-strained neck muscles.

"Mr. Merrill," Price said. "The sensitivity of these photographs is usually such that we could pinpoint an abnormal generation of infrared-sensitive heat."

"But we're not looking for heat, we're looking for sealed canisters of nuclear waste materials," Merrill insisted. He was obviously aggravated.

"Exactly," Carl said. "But nuclear materials generate a modest level of heat even in a dormant state. There is a chance these photos could give us at least some reference point to start."

"Are you trying to tell me that some satellite thousands of miles out in space has the ability to find twelve tiny canisters of nuclear by-product on the ass-end of a tractor-trailer?" Merrill asked.

"A good summation, Mr. Merrill," Marc said.

"Shit, I can't believe that," Merrill said, and he pushed himself away from the table, shaking his head all the while.

"Believe him, Mr. Merrill," Price said. "The Russians have been doing it for over a decade."

"No shit?"

"No shit," Carl said.

"You see, Mr. Merrill, even as small as those canisters are, there are radiation traces. These traces show up as tracks on the photos. Essentially, they record on film as heat glitches with just a shade more resolution and distinction."

"Then why don't we just let the satellite find that shit

and send a few boys in to recover it? If it's that good, the rest of us can just pack up and go to the house," Merrill said.

"We've oversimplified it, I'm afraid. Look at the glitches." Marc pointed to the hundreds of white splotches on the photos. "Each of those spots is a potential radiation emission."

"There are hundreds on these photos. But some are whiter than others. Why is that?" Merrill asked.

"Relative intensity of the source," Price said.

"We couldn't possibly eliminate all of these places in the time frame we are dealing with. Is this just another dead-end street?" Merrill asked.

"Not exactly," Marc said. "Through a reasonable process of elimination, we can narrow our hunting grounds. Some of the glitches are prominent because of the intrinsic heat dissipated by cities, buildings, and such."

"Hey, guys, I don't want to come off as the eternal pessimist, but California is a mighty big state. And besides that, we don't even know the stuff is still in this state," Merrill said.

"Step number one in the elimination process," Marc said. "According to the police report in the case folder, the truck driver was still warm when his body was found. That means he couldn't have been dead very long. It also means the rig couldn't have gone very far without someone seeing it. To date, we have no reports of anyone seeing Artlie Anders's rig. I think we need to confine our search efforts to areas within this perimeter." Marc drew a red pencil circle around an area on the map indicating the mountains of Northern California.

"I agree," Price said. "What Mr. Lee says makes sense."

"Yeah, but where do we start looking?" Carl said.

"First places first," Marc said. "Take three days of

photographs, make in-depth comparisons of the glitches within this circle, and let's got retrieve our stolen waste."

"It sounds too damn simple," Merrill said.

"Not if you don't overcomplicate it," Marc replied with a smile.

"I like it," Price said, a broad smile etched across his boyish face.

"Okay, looks like it's showtime," Marc said. "By the way, where's the rig?"

"Through that door," Price said.

"Good. I'd like to take a few minutes' break from these photos and check it out. How about you, Carl?"

"Sounds good." Carl stood from the table. "We need to load our gear, too."

"Do you guys see what time it is?" Merrill asked. "We've got less than twenty-four hours until these psychopaths threatened to open a canister. Can we make it by then?"

"We can try," Marc said, and he left the office and went into the hangar.

———

"I'm going to check in on Marcus while you finish getting your things together," Brittin Crain said.

"I won't be long. Do we have time to go by my house and let me get a few personal items?" Jill asked.

"If we don't linger," Crain replied. "The plane leaves in two hours. You know how confusing it is at DFW. It may take an hour to get through the lines for boarding."

"I'll hurry," Jill said as Crain disappeared through the doorway.

Crain stopped for a moment and exchanged idle conversation with the police guards in the living room area of the underground safe-room. When the conversation ended, he knocked gently on the door to Marcus Lee's room.

The door opened and a nurse appeared. "Brittin, how are you? Come on in," Linda Morgan said. The slightly overweight nurse stepped back from the door and waited for Crain to enter.

As he stepped through the doorway into Marcus Lee's room, Crain felt an uneasiness in his stomach, an almost nauseating feeling. It was seeing the man flat on his back and sleeping in a violence-induced sleep that caused the sick feeling.

Crain had known the big Texan for almost as long as he could remember. He had seen Leeco Freight Lines when the big rigs rolled America's highways and the company was a thriving private enterprise. And to see Marcus the way he was now caused a great deal of personal pain. He knew how Marc must have felt when he had to deal with his father's condition . . . the sleep from which awakening was uncertain at best. Crain likened it to seeing a mighty warship condemned to mothballs after a gallant life at sea.

Perhaps, Crain thought, the day would come when there would be an awakening, a resurrection, and Marcus Lee would be among them again.

"Any change we should know about?" Brittin asked as he faced the nurse.

"Vitals are normal, heart is strong, respiration is excellent, the ear is completely healed. Poor man just can't wake up, that's all," Linda Morgan said sadly.

"It's just such a waste—a damn shame."

"I know."

"Do you mind if I spend a few minutes alone with him? I don't know when I'll get back here again," Crain said.

"Sure, I'll wait out in the living room. I could use the break anyway."

"Thanks."

Linda Morgan left the room and closed the door. Crain stepped closer to the bed and, like others before him, started a one-way conversation with the sleeping Texas trucking giant.

"Marcus, I think you'd be proud. No, I know you would be. Marc has stepped into a world where few, if any, men have gone before. This fiasco at Leeco, this war, has changed life for all of us. It will never be like it was before . . . but you'd be proud because you son is standing tall. He's fighting for the cause—he and Carl. Leeco is going to make it. How do I know that? The president of the United States told me so himself. Can you believe that? It's true. The president of the United States assured me, Marc, and Carl that Leeco Freight Lines would sustain. He's even sending in some of his own personal people to operate it until you wake up. Isn't that amazing?"

Crain stopped talking, shrugged his shoulders, and wiped a tiny tear from the corner of his eye. He stared at Marcus Lee and wondered where their lives would go from here.

"Hey, you take care now. I've got to go. Jill is with me for a while and she'll be all right. Marc will come see you soon. We're going to leave you here where it's safe until we're all sure the war has really ended. You'll have constant care. That's about all Marc or any of us can do now. You're a man of great will. We all know that. If you can hear me now, Marcus, make yourself get better. There's a new world waiting for you out here and we're all pulling for you. Come join us."

Crain touched Marcus Lee's hand and walked to the door. He opened it and left the room without looking back.

Marcus Lee's hand twitched and his fingers moved. He opened his eyes, his head unmoving, and he looked at the strange place surrounding him. His mind didn't understand what he saw, so he closed his eyes again and slipped back into the sleep.

———

The compound yard was active now with several dozen men. The smell of woodsmoke filled the crisp morning air. A line had formed beside one of the shabby barracks. Inside, each man took a plate, filled it with food, and sat at one of the long rough wooden tables. A mixture of conversations filled the room, some in native Japanese, and others in perfect English.

Across the compound, Izumi Shimada lifted the handset on the portable cellular telephone.

"Good morning to you, also, Mori Osamu. Yes, Nagai is here with me. One moment, please," Izumi said as he handed the handset to Nagai Soseki.

"Yes, Mori," Soseki said as he placed the handset to his head.

"We must prepare to move the material across the country," Osamu said. "Do you have the materials-handling suits?"

"Yes, they are secure in the tractor-trailer rig," Soseki said.

"Good. Have some volunteers suit up and prepare two canisters for transit. If the government fails to make the initial payment, as I am inclined to believe will be the case, we must follow through with our plan."

"Understood, Mori," Soseki said.

"You must also accept two volunteers to drive the rig, perhaps two of the older men. It will be for the honor of our homeland and our ancestors that the two who feel chosen enter into a kamikaze mission. They will be heroes who will earn a place before Buddha."

"Do you really believe the American government will

fail to deliver our resources? Surely they are not that foolish," Soseki said.

"It is likely. We must show this country we are sincere. We must teach them how harmful radiation really is. The Friends of Humanity have a responsibility to ourselves and mankind."

"It is an honorable purpose, Mori Osamu," Soseki said.

"If we accomplish nothing more than new regulations for the transportation of radioactive death, we have given our lives heroically. What we do is tame compared to the free-lance death *real* terrorists could invoke with radioactive materials. The mere thought depresses me."

"It causes me great sorrow that we must take lives to keep more lives from being lost," Soseki said.

"I also share that sorrow, Nagai. But those of us who work within the government have long since learned that change frequently requires radical measures to achieve the desired effect. We must gain the attention of the American people. The deaths of the few can sustain the lives of the many if they will only heed the warnings. It is worth it, Nagai. It is worth it."

CHAPTER SEVEN

Marc and Carl scrutinized the rig Agent Harrison had made available for them. It was an almost new conventional Class 8 Peterbilt with a forty-eight-foot Strick trailer. The Peterbilt was fire-engine red with a double sleeper and wind foiler.

"This will work," Marc said.

"I like the color," Carl replied.

"The communications equipment is in place and the ramps are in the back. It's a good start," said Marc.

"Let's check out the Jeep," Carl said.

Marc and Carl walked to a new black Jeep Cherokee parked in the hangar beside the rig. Two five-eighths wave vertical antennas were mounted on the top, both base-loaded with stainless steel whips. One was for ultrahigh frequencies and the other for very high frequencies. A communications console was mounted on the transmission hump. The vehicle was four-wheel drive with an automatic transmission and four-liter six-cylinder engine. The spare tire was mounted on a swing-out rack attached to the back bumper and quarter-panel.

"Nice," Marc commented.

"Are the radios what you wanted?" Carl asked.

"They'll work. I'll do something a little differently when we go for a permanent four-by-four. We can make some notes and get them off to Harrison before we leave here."

"The Jeep is smaller than the Ram, so it will fit into the back of the rig a little easier. I like that," Carl said.

"Yeah," Marc said. "I think the Jeep will do anything the Ram could do. It might even get in a few tight places the Ram couldn't. I miss the old Ram, it had served me well; but I can get used to one of these. How about you?"

"Personally, I like the four-wheel drive system on the Jeep better. Face it, Jeep has always made a hell of a war machine."

The door from the office to the hangar opened and Gary Merrill shouted.

"Mr. Lee, Mr. Browne, I've got something for you."

"Be right there," Marc said.

Marc and Carl went into the office alcove where Merrill, Harrison, and Price were waiting, but only after taking one more affectionate look at their new equipment.

"What's up?" Carl asked.

"We just got the FBI lab results from the transmitter unit from the telephone booth. It's interesting," Merrill said.

"How so?" Marc asked.

"Here, take a look for yourself." Merrill handed the fax copy to Marc.

Marc took the papers and read through them quickly. He handed the report to Carl.

"What's your consensus?" Merrill asked.

"The person or persons responsible for this are very efficient. There were no fingerprints, nothing to indicate who is responsible. The circuitry is high-tech state of the art and amazingly effective. And the fact that the device was homebrew—that tells me something," Marc said.

"Like these people are damned intelligent?" Merrill said.

"Exactly," Marc said. "They know what they're doing, at least with electronics. I don't think we're dealing with stereotypical terrorists here. And that integrated circuit op-amp chip, it's ultrahigh tech. The device is so new, it's never been exported from Japan. It's an ultralow noise and super high-gain operational amplifier. I've read about it in trade journals. I'm not aware of any Americans who have ever seen one, much less had the opportunity to use one. The potential uses are so vast, the Japanese are keeping it for themselves. If these people got their hands on it, they must have an inside link with Japanese engineering firms."

"Are you saying the Japanese may be involved in this?" Merrill asked.

"Not necessarily the Japanese government. Maybe just some radical faction. It could even be a corporate plot for God knows what purpose," Marc said.

"You mean we may be barking up the wrong tree so far?" Carl said.

"Maybe. The Vietnamese apology business may just be a decoy to throw us off the real track," Marc said.

"Do you really think the Japanese could be involved in this?" asked Merrill.

"I don't know," Marc said. "I'm not saying they are involved, but someone has a connection somewhere inside Japan or they never could have gotten their hands on that chip. Like I said, it's in common usage over there, but it's never been exported. Right now, it's the only link we have."

"It doesn't make sense. Japanese companies own hundreds of American corporations and they're buying up half of Hawaii. Why would they do something this crazy and jeopardize a good relationship?"

"Maybe we've missed the real motive," Marc said.

"Like what?" asked Carl.

"Could be it isn't money these folks are after."

"But that's all they've asked for so far—money and an apology to the people of Vietnam," Merrill said.

"Mr. Lee may be right," Price said. "Maybe they don't want money. Maybe they want attention."

Merrill seemed puzzled. "Why would someone steal lethal nuclear waste just to get attention?"

"Think about it for a minute," Marc said. "Let's slip into some simple what-ifs. Suppose the apology thing is a decoy. Suppose a Japanese radical faction is involved, perhaps with help from stateside sympathizers. Where does that leave us?"

"In a hell of a mess," Carl said.

"In more ways than one," Merrill added.

"Granted, but think of this. Who would know better than the Japanese people the real ramifications of radiation poisoning and radiation sickness? When we hit Hiroshima and Nagasaki, there were literally countless deaths. The Japanese have seen the results firsthand."

"But what does that prove? What do they have to gain? Face it, to the Japanese economy, fifty million dollars doesn't mean anything," Merrill said.

"You're missing the point, Gary," Marc said. "Maybe it isn't the money. Maybe it's vengeance for what we did to them or maybe even some sick way of trying to forewarn us of things to come."

"What are you saying?" Merrill asked.

"Look at the facts. First, why would they hit a truck for nuclear waste? There are Japanese engineers, technicians, and scientists working in every aspect of American business perfectly legally and openly—at the invitation of American companies. That includes the nuclear family of enterprises. Hell, they could take over a nuclear electrical generation facility if they wanted it, or even a submarine. Why waste product and why a truck?" Marc asked.

"Could be we can't see the constellation because we're too busy looking at the stars," Price said.

"That's right," Marc said. "Look who the call went

to—the EPA. We've been missing it all along. These people don't want money, they want our attention."

"Wait a minute," Merrill said. "The guy who heads the L.A. office of the EPA, the guy who took the call from the thieves—shit! We've overlooked the obvious."

"What about his?" asked Marc.

"His name is Jim Yasunari. He's Japanese-American."

"Is there any reason to believe he's involved?" asked Carl.

"He's the one who got the call," Marc said. "It's probably just a coincidence—if our scenario is anywhere close to being true."

"I'll have the bureau initiate a complete background investigation on him immediately. I'll see what he's been involved in and even find out the last time he took a piss, if you want me to," Merrill said.

"Do it," Marc said. "While you're at it, run down any high-tech, nuclear-related businesses with overseas interests, get a list of researchers and physicists on the West Coast, and find any trucking firms or other transportation entities that are owned by Japanese or persons with Japanese connections. It's a long shot, but I have a gut feeling about this."

"It's done," Merrill said.

"Captain, how quickly can have have planes in the air?" asked Marc.

"Five minutes," Price replied. "Why?"

"Take everything you have that will fly and is equipped with radiation-sensing equipment and get it airborne. Make it look like a training mission. The true nature of our search cannot leave this room. One leak to the general public or the news media, and we'll blow this entire operation. If we blow it, you can bet your ass innocent people are going to die."

"Got it," Price replied.

"And Captain, cover every square inch of this country west of the Rocky Mountains," Marc added.

"Done," Price said.

"While you guys handle that end of things, Carl and I are going to Northern California in the rig. I think I'm on to another angle, but we need to check it out ourselves. If we score, I'll contact you by radio. We can all stay linked by the Defense Department's radio repeater link. That will give us direct contact with the command center in Washington. If one of us hits, we can all move in and close this thing down for good."

"We don't have much time left," Merrill said. "I sure hope we're on to the right angle."

"If we're wrong, a lot of Americans are going to learn what the Japanese learned over forty years ago. We have to find these people and stop them before death puts on a new face in this country," Marc said.

———

It had been over an hour since Marc and Carl started rolling the Peterbilt rig over Route 58 to Bakersfield. The city made famous by country music artists and their songs was behind them now. They were nearing the entry ramp to Interstate 5. Conversation had been light and the time had been spent with Marc driving and Carl making notes for the design of the overroad rig the president had promised to deliver upon receipt of their specifications.

Carl laid his pencil and notepad aside. He looked to his friend as Marc shifted through the gears, gliding the Peterbilt onto the ramp and into the flow of traffic heading north.

"You drive this thing like you were wearing it," Carl said.

"When I'm driving, it gives me time to think. It helps unclutter my mind."

"I guess we'll be getting a lot of road time before we're through if this radiation doesn't take us out."

"I guess," Marc said.

"Where are we going, or should I even ask?"

"I didn't want those other guys to know what I had in mind, but it all seems so simple."

"What?"

"If a Japanese radical group is involved in this extortion scheme, I think I know where they'll be."

"Where?"

"Get those California maps and the satellite photos out of my travel bag," Marc said.

Carl rummaged through Marc's leather travel pack and finally came out with maps and photos. "Okay, now what?"

"If it is a Japanese terrorist group, I want you to think about something. During World War Two, there were a great many Americans of Japanese descent living in the United States. When it became obvious the Imperial Japanese government was an enemy, the American government ordered a roundup of all known Japanese on the West Coast. The Japanese-American population in California was vast. The government constructed encampments to house these people and keep them under a watchful eye. It wasn't fair, but it was wartime. Some of those same facilities are still in existence today. It's a hunch, but I think we might find our stolen nuclear waste in one of the old abandoned encampments."

"And what happens if Japanese terrorists aren't involved?" asked Carl.

"Then we're shit out of luck and it's back to square one," Marc said coldly.

"Where are these abandoned camps?" Carl asked.

"According to the information I have, there were three of them in Northern California."

"It's still a big damn place. What makes you think we can find them in time to stop this craziness?"

"The process of elimination and those satellite photos," Marc said confidently. "Open the photos and I'll show you."

Carl unfolded the satellite fax photos and laid them on his lap.

"Okay, get a surveillance photo from last Sunday and lay it beside the ones from Monday," Marc said.

Carl checked the date etched in the corner of each photograph and arranged them side by side.

"Now, pull those old maps out and look for the three areas I circled in red. That indicates the position of the abandoned government camps, at least approximately."

"Okay, what are we looking for?"

"These areas are mountainous and sparsely populated. There should be little or no indication of active radiation or heat showing up on the photos. Look at the Monday evening photos first."

Carl made the comparisons, mumbling all the while. After a few minutes he stopped. "I don't see anything. No, wait a minute. Here, on a place that would be just barely inside one of the red circles."

"What is it?"

"A white dot about the size of a pin head," Carl said.

"I'll stop the rig. I want to take a look," Marc said. He signaled a right turn and slowed the rig to the shoulder of the Interstate highway. Once the Peterbilt was stopped, he switched on his four-way flasher and leaned over to the maps.

"Is it anything?" Carl asked.

"Could be. Let's take a look at Sunday's pictures," Marc said as he fumbled through the papers. "Yeah, look here on Sunday. It's not showing."

"You're right. Have we hit a home run?"

"I don't know. Dig up Tuesday's photo."

Carl dug through the stack of fax photos and found Tuesday. "Here you go," he said.

"Yeah, yeah, look, the white glitch is also on Tuesday's picture. This may be something."

"Man, you knew this before we left Edwards, didn't you?"

"It was a hunch, yes. Why?"

"Shit, man, that's my question. Why didn't you tell the others?"

"Because if I'm right, I don't want the federal bureaucracy coming in like a herd of horses and screwing everything up. I think we'll work better by ourselves."

"Okay, then what are we going to do if we find those damned canisters at this place or even somewhere else?"

"We're going to steal them back. Then we'll kick ass and take names," Marc said with a grin.

"What? You're shittin' me, ain't you?"

"Nope. I'm deadly serious." Marc kicked the Peterbilt into low gear and headed out into the traffic again.

"That's what I was afraid you'd say," Carl said as he shook his head in disbelieve. "You're not going to be happy until you get us killed, are you?"

"I haven't yet, have I?"

"No, but it damn sure ain't because you haven't tried."

"I have a plan. It's almost like the one we used in Iran a few years ago. Tell me what you think. . . ."

Marc drove the Peterbilt as he continued to outline the plan. If they were fortunate enough to find the stolen canisters of nuclear waste, he wanted to be ready. The hours turned into miles and countless towns left behind them. The Peterbilt roared and diesel smoke churned skyward, leaving a thin black trail in the slipstream.

The conversation inside the cab left the assault plan and slipped into the plans for their permanent overroad rig. They tossed ideas back and forth, Carl scribbling notes with each new brainstorm. They had been on the open road for ten hours, but the time had passed quickly. The Delta Warriors had made only one stop for fuel and a meal. Several times during the day, Carl had called in to the temporary command center at Edwards Air Force Base. The search teams had found nothing from the sky, and Merrill was awaiting further information on Jim Yasunari of the EPA.

Night had fallen over Northern California, and the bright sun of the day had been replaced by scattered stars dotting the deep black sky. The Halogen headlights on the front of the Peterbilt ate through the darkness, illuminating the way to what Marc and Carl suspected would be their next battlefield. Except for the constant chatter on the CB radio, the cab of the mighty Peterbilt had been silent for an hour.

"The turnoff we're looking for should be a mile and a half ahead," Carl said, breaking the silence.

"Good. I sure will be glad to get out and stretch my legs."

"I second that."

"What say we find a place near the interstate and leave the rig? I think we can be more effective in the Jeep," Marc said.

"I'm for that. Most of the firepower is in the Jeep, anyway. The maps indicate some rugged terrain. I have a feeling we'll be running the Cherokee through the paces."

"You'll be impressed with it, I think."

The sign indicating the exit appeared and Marc slowed the rig, signaling the turn. He stopped at the end of the exit ramp, then made a left turn under the interstate highway.

An old abandoned gasoline service station sat within a half mile of the exit on the left side of the narrow two-lane road. Marc almost missed it, but he slowed quickly and pulled the rig into the parking lot. The night was unusually

dark and the area exceptionally desolate. The overroad rig
had exclusive reign on the road. As the headlights of the
Peterbilt panned the parking lot, Marc noticed stands of
knee-high dead grass protruding through the cracks in the
pavement. The roof on the old building was partially caved
in and the windows were boarded over—protection from
vandals, Marc assumed. The owners had used good judgment, because the lot was littered with fist-sized rocks and
broken bottles. The boards covering the windows and doors
to the old station were scarred with graffiti, the most
prominent of which was a bright red spray-painted heart
with white letters that read, JASON LOVES AMANDA—1986.

"Looks like a good place to leave the rig for a few hours,"
Marc said.

"If the local thugs don't pelt it with rocks and bottles or
lovebirds don't try to build a nest in it, maybe it can survive
here awhile," Carl said, and he laughed.

Marc turned the rig around in the parking lot and
stopped, with the front of the Peterbilt facing back into the
highway. "Let's unload the Cherokee and get with it. Oh,
don't forget the maps."

"Yeah, I got 'em," Carl replied.

Marc and Carl met at the rear of the trailer. Carl held
the four-D-cell Mag-Lite while Marc unlocked the trailer
hasp lock. Once that was done, they opened the doors and
immediately set the ramps to drive the Cherokee from the
trailer.

Carl drove the Cherokee down the ramps while Marc
assembled three additional field boxes of 5.56mm military
ball ammunition. "Damn, Harrison did deliver," Marc said
as Carl walked beside him.

"What's that?" asked Carl.

"The Winchester nine-millimeter Silvertips I asked for
to use in the Berettas and the Uzis," Mark said as he
pressed the last round into one of the Beretta's magazines

and slipped it up the well of the automatic pistol. He worked the slide back and let it slam closed, stripping the top round from the magazine."

"Good," Carl said as he took his own Beretta from his waistband holster. "That's a badass hollow-point round. A lot of cops have gotten smart and they're carrying these now. But then, you knew that, didn't you?"

"Yes. For a factory round, it's probably the best we can get for our purposes. It will do until we can get somewhere and roll a few thousand of our own. I still like to customize the load for the gun," Marc said.

"Weapons are all secure in the Cherokee. I'll load some extra magazines while we're on the way." Carl hesitated. "Brother, do you really think we'll find that stolen stuff in this camp?"

"We'll know in a little while, won't we?" Marc's face was already hardening, an indication he was mentally preparing for a worst-case scenario.

"You boys just freeze right where you are if you don't wanna be breathin' out the back of your heads," came a slow, drawling, yet gruff voice from behind Marc and Carl. The white light of a spotlight illuminated the Cherokee and the doors on the Strick trailer like daylight. "Now," the voice continued, "just lay them guns to the ground real nice and easy-like. You try any of that citified cute shit and when I finish with your heads, I'm gonna shoot your asses off."

CHAPTER EIGHT

Nagai Soseki directed the work inside the cave as dozens of men hoisted two canisters of nuclear waste from the stolen flatbed truck. The heavy titanium steel containers were moved to the enclosed trailer Soseki had driven into the compound. A delicate and sophisticated system of makeshift block-and-tackle pulley assemblies affixed to lengths of heavy woven nylon rope served as the transfer assembly line. Hand-hewn redwood timbers, most older than the men themselves, supported the complicated rope system. The work had taken hours once the elaborate trolleylike system was in place. The workers were extremely careful in handling the waste product although the canisters were superior transportation devices capable of withstanding extreme abuse. Still, Soseki—his vast knowledge of nuclear energy second to few other living nuclear physicists—believed in extravagant precaution. Under no circumstances would he allow the radioactive death stored inside the containers to be released before the purpose of his mission dictated it a necessity.

Should that necessity occur, Soseki had rationalized to his personal satisfaction that death to even a few thousand would be justified if the sacrifice could eventually save millions. And without the efforts of Friends of Humanity, the eventuality of the deaths of millions from a catastrophic nuclear accident was not mere conjectured speculation, it was a certainty. Soseki, as did the others of his following, believed transportation regulations were too lax and safeguards were too few. For years the dancers had swept freely across the floor of the North American continent, carefree of the cost of nuclear domination. But all the while, the fiddler kept the score. And one day when it was least expected, he would demand that which he was due. When that day came, payback would make hell seem like a blessing.

Shadows danced on the rock walls of the cave, given birth by evenly spaced kerosene lanterns suspended from iron hangers driven into the stone. The workers manipulated the canisters, and from a distance they looked like ants moving large crumb of bread.

"Nagai," Izumi Shimada said. "Do you believe the American government officials will succumb to our demands?"

"One way or another, yes," Soseki replied. We have thrown them completely off track with our threats. While they comb the crevices of Los Angeles for these canisters, our drivers will be on their way to Salt Lake City. Many will die if the government fails to act."

"Yes, and tomorrow morning, Mori Osamu will arrive with another highway rig. Perhaps our alternate plan will add an altogether new glow to the casinos of Las Vegas," Izumi said.

"Indeed, my young compatriot. You can bet on it."

———

"Are you sure?" Agent Gary Merrill asked the agent on the telephone. He had returned to his office in suburban Los Angeles. It was after eight o'clock in the evening and all of the employees had gone home except him. Every field agent available was on overtime, scraping the sludge from the bottom of the criminal pit and looking for a lead. He was alone and he liked that. It gave him time for thought, and right now thought was what the case was demanding. "How is it possible that a man can be a regional director of the Environmental Protection Agency and not have a complete personnel file on government computers?"

"Beats hell out of me, boss," the agent replied. "But Jim Yasunari's file does not exist in any of the Untied States government computer records."

"Shit!" Merrill said. "How about payroll? Does the son of a bitch show up on the payroll system?"

"Yep, but that's about the only place," the agent replied. "Treasury, Social Security, and the IRS all have him down by employee number or Social Security number, but that's it."

"Did you try NCIC and Interpol?" Merrill asked.

"A whopping big zero. The guy has no prints on file and no previous criminal history."

"My mother-in-law isn't that clean," Merrill shouted. "Everybody has something somewhere. Get whatever manpower you need and keep digging until you find it."

"Right, boss," the agent replied.

"And while you're looking, get a surveillance detail on his ass. I want to know every move this man makes. I want to know who he talks to and where he goes. I want to know who he's sleeping with and what he does when he isn't isolated in the ivory thrones of the EPA."

"Consider it done."

"I mean it. If this guy has a pimple on the cheeks of his ass I want to know about it. Is that clear?"

"Affirmative. What's your gut tellin' you, boss? Is Yasunari involved?"

"It's the only shot we've got. Right now, we'll take it," Merrill said.

"Okay, we're moving," the agent said, he hung up the telephone.

Merrill slammed the telephone handset back into the cradle and reached into his pocket for a cigarette. He found the wrinkled pack and removed the last bent cigarette from it. He tapped the filter end on the table two or three times and then placed it between his lips. He fumbled for the disposable lighter in his jacket pocket. Once he found it, he flipped the wheel on the Bic and lit the cigarette. He took a long, soothing draw and blew the smoke toward the ceiling. In a single motion, he laid the burning cigarette in an ashtray in front of him and reached for the telephone.

When Merrill heard the dial tone, he punched in the number he wanted. A woman answered.

"Hi, honey. Don't wait supper for me. It looks like another long night," Merrill said.

"Is it that bad again?" Shirley Merrill asked. After twelve years of marriage and two children, she had become accustomed to her husband's second marriage to his job. A late night was more routine than unusual.

"I have to review some tapes from this NRC mess. As soon as I'm finished with that, I'll head on home."

"Any idea how long that might be?"

"Two, maybe two and a half hours—at the most. Did you have a good day?"

"It was nice. Have you had a hectic one?"

"That's an understatement. Listen, I'll grab a burger or something on the way in so you don't have a mess to clean in the morning. Will that be okay?"

"Suit yourself, but I don't mind if you want something warm. I'll keep it in the oven until you get here."

"Thanks, sweetheart, but I'll just pick something up."

"Okay."

"Listen, kiss the kids for me, and tell them I love them and I'll see them in the morning. Okay?"

"Sure."

"Hey, don't sound so dejected, sweet lady. I love you, too."

"I love you."

"See you in a couple hours. Bye."

"Good-bye."

Merrill hung up the telephone and reached across his desk for his portable cassette player/recorder. He picked up the burning cigarette and inhaled the last tobacco before the filter started to burn. He stubbed it out in the ashtray and looked at the label on the cassette tape beside the recorder. It was a tape of the conversation between Jim Yasunari and the terrorist caller. He stuck the tape into the machine and pressed the play button. As the tape started, he leaned back in his chair and cupped his hands against his mouth.

When the taped conversation had ended, he rewound it and played it again. For thirty minutes, he repeated the procedure. Each time he listened with more discriminating ears, and each time he found nothing new. There were no clues, nothing tipped a hand or pointed a finger. There was no distinct accent or inflection to the caller's voice, no unusual vocabulary. It was too bland, too perfect.

Merrill had finally bored himself with the tape. He ejected it from the machine and laid it aside on his desk. He picked up a stack of reports from the field agents and thumbed through them. One finally caught his attention because it had a cassette tape attached to it.

Merrill read the information on the subject, a Nagai Soseki, Ph. D. According to the report, Soseki was one of the nation's foremost and respected authorities on nuclear energy. He had come to America as a child and all ties with his homeland had been severed. He had been granted citizenship while still a child. Soseki had gained a professional reputation for being assertive and bluntly outspoken with his opinions on nuclear safety. He lectured at the

Davis campus of the University of California and was a dominant figure in the nuclear research facility there. The investigating agent had been unable to speak with Soseki directly because Soseki had been out on sick leave for several days. As a verification of his efforts, the agent had purchased an audio cassette of Soseki's lectures from the campus bookstore. The agent attached a note to the tape that indicated some of Soseki's lectures were poignant and precautionary.

The note aroused Merrill's interest. He slipped the tape from its box and slid it into the cassette player. When he hit the play button and leaned back in his chair, he yearned for another cigarette, but he settled for clasped hands behind his head instead.

The lecture started and Merrill jumped straight up from his chair. At first he thought his ears were deceiving him. He stopped the tape player, ejected the tape, and slid the recording of the telephone call into the machine.

He listened carefully for a moment, then switched the tapes again. He repeated the procedure six or seven times. Then he knew: It was the same person.

"Holy shit!" he said aloud, though no one was there to hear him.

Merrill quickly gathered the tapes, the report, and the tape player. He ran for the door and his car. He had to get the information to Marc and Carl and the search team.

Merrill reached his car and tossed everything into the front seat. He grabbed the red light on the floorboard and placed it on top of his car, hit the siren switch, and headed for Edwards Air Force Base.

Merrill was less than ten blocks from his office when he entered an intersection against a red traffic light. He didn't see the eighteen-wheeler until he was less than a car length from it. His foot reached the brake pedal just as the government car crashed beneath the trailer of the rig. The top of the car from the door handles upward peeled back like a poorly opened can of tuna. A microinstant later, the car and the rig erupted into a gyrating mass of flaming death.

———

"Now, you two oversized assholes turn around real slow. You blink your eyes the wrong way and me and Jake's gonna rearrange your nostrils," came the gruff voice from the darkness.

Marc and Carl did as they were told. The bright white spotlight blinded them. They could see the source of the light but the intensity was too great to determine how many men were beside it.

A large silhouette appeared from the darkness and stepped into the light. The first thing Carl could make out was the double-barreled shotgun in the man's hands.

"Now just what do you dickheads think you're doing out here with them guns and shit?" the unidentified man asked. The tone and texture of his voice indicated he was a man of maturity and probably in his sixties.

"I guess that depends on who's askin'," Marc replied coldly.

"Who's askin' is the son of a bitch with this shotgun leveled at you, smart shit."

"Well, since you put it that way," Carl said, "we're just gearin' up to go huntin'."

"Yeah, huntin' my hairy ass. Ain't no huntin' season open now. You boys is poachers, ain't you?"

Marc started to tell the man they were hunting old farts carrying shotguns, but his better judgment prevailed and he decided it would be better to play along, considering the circumstances. "Actually, mister, we're government agents and we're up here looking for some stolen radioactive nuclear materials we think have fallen into the wrong hands," Marc said, figuring the truth seemed so bizarre that the old man wouldn't fall for it anyway.

"Yeah, sure you are. And I'm a long-dick camel. Now who the hell are you?"

"I'm serious. My identification is in my shirt pocket. Can I give it to you?" Marc asked.

The man hesitated for a long moment. "Okay, Jake, come on out and go get that there I.D. and let's see who these peckerheads really are. I'll cover you."

Another man, previously unseen by Marc and Carl, stepped into the light. He started toward the Delta Warriors, moving slowly and carefully. He, too, was carrying a shotgun. As he got a little closer, Marc could make out the trimmings of a uniform of some type.

"Man, you're gonna get us killed. You don't have a damn I.D.," Carl whispered.

"I know that and you know that, but these mental midgets don't," Marc replied.

"What are you gonna do when he gets to you?" asked Carl nervously.

"Take him down. You duck behind the Cherokee when I deck him. I'll hold him up for a shield while you get the other one."

"What the hell are you two chatterin' about? Shut the hell up till Jake gets that I.D. you say you got."

Marc and Carl were silent, their attention focused on the silhouette of the man moving toward them. When Jake was ten feet from Marc and Carl, he stopped.

Marc could see the shotgun now. It was a twelve-gauge Mossberg 500 Persuader. Even in the blinding light of the spotlight, the business end of the eighteen-inch barrel looked like a water pipe. He could also tell more about the uniform now. Although Jake wore it in disarray, Marc could see it was a brown and tan sheriff's uniform. A silver five-point star was pinned just above the left breast pocket. Jake also wore a Sam Browne gunbelt with a revolver on his right hip.

Jake was a slight man, standing no more than five-feet-eight and probably not over 140 pounds. Marc noticed a slight quivering of the shotgun barrel, an indication that Jake was extremely nervous and scared. And Marc knew there was nothing more potentially dangerous than a nervous man with his finger on a trigger.

"Okay, hotshot," Jake said with a slight tremble in his voice. "Slip that I.D. out of your pocket with your left hand. And don't be a fool, or me and this here scattergun will splatter you all over this parking lot."

Jake was trying to come off hard, but Marc knew that inside the man was turning to jelly.

"Don't get too excited with that shotgun when I reach for the wallet," Marc said.

"Just do it!" Jake shouted.

Marc reached into his breast pocket and found his nylon wallet. He was thankful he had moved it there when he and Carl stopped at the truckstop several hours before. It had become uncomfortable sitting on it while he drove the rig for so many hours.

"Now, toss it over to me," Jake said when Marc produced the wallet in his hand.

Marc complied with Jake's order. But instead of tossing accurately, Marc let the wallet fall short. It landed halfway between him and Jake.

"You don't throw for shit," Jake said, and he eased toward the wallet lying on the cracked parking lot pavement.

"Sorry," Marc said as he watched every movement Jake made and started his mental timing.

Jake held the shotgun with one hand now. He knelt slowly to the ground, his eyes fixed on Marc and the shotgun leveled at Marc's head. Jake fumbled around, feeling the pavement with his free hand, but he couldn't find the wallet. His eyes left Marc for a split second.

That's all it took. Marc flew forward, his body parallel to the ground in a flying scissor kick. Jake didn't have time to react before Marc's feet slammed into his chest. Jake fell back, but Marc was on his feet and his left arm grabbed Jake's shirt. The shotgun fell harmlessly to the pavement as Marc spun Jake around with a hard jerk and put his neck in a hammerlock.

Marc grabbed Jake's revolver with his right hand and placed it to the side of Jake's head while holding the trembling man tightly against his own body.

Carl had disappeared into the darkness, his huge black hand sweeping up a Beretta as he rolled into the night.

"Bastards!" the gruff old man yelled, and his voice was covered by the sound of a shotgun blast.

———

"I am seeking two volunteers to drive this truck to Salt Lake City, Utah," Nagai Soseki said to the men gathered around the flatbed rig inside the huge cave. "It will be an effort for all humanity. Those who are chosen by the spirit of Buddha will reign forever with honor as true kamikaze. A death more honorable cannot be found in this foreign land. Who is chosen?"

Every hand in the kerosene-scented cave shot into the air at the same time.

"We are comprised of very honorable men, and I therefore am honored," Soseki said. "Let us share some rice wine and I shall soon make a selection of the men who will receive this most noble honor."

The loyal Friends of Humanity sat together in the center of the cave's earthen floor. Soseki, as the leader and the one deserving of the most respect, opened the first bottle of *sake*. He poured a drink into a small paper cup and passed the bottle around. Each man poured a drink of warm rice wine and held the cup still until Soseki sipped his.

The revelry lasted for an hour and finally Soseki stood, his hands up to indicate quiet. The cave fell from constant chatter to deathly silence.

"Tomorrow morning, Mori Osamu will arrive with another truck. We will then move a second cargo of radioactive elements to another city, Las Vegas. When our canisters are in place, we will unveil our new demands for the so far deaf ears of the United States government. If the people in positions of responsibility fail to heed our warnings, we will then release the radioactive menace upon the population. Once our canisters have been opened, we will contact the electronic news media and verbalize our stand. We will be heard and we will save mankind from the poisonous abject apathy that is rampant in this country."

Soseki stopped speaking, his voice drowned by the cheers and applause of the men in front of him. The interruption lasted more than a minute, and then silence resumed.

"We will see the changes we desire come forth. We will cause the forces of the split atom to work for the good of mankind so that we may assure a world of prosperity and peace for our children and all the children of the world."

Again, there were cheers and applause.

"I have made a decision in honor of the old and the new. The oldest man present and the youngest man present will share the honor of driving the first tractor-trailer to leave the compound. The second oldest and the second youngest will be given the honor of transporting the next shipment to Las Vegas. It is the knowledge of age and the ambition of youth that must carry our purpose through to finalization."

There were more cheers, more alcohol-fed revelry.

Soseki raised his full cup above his head. "Please, silence."

The cave became still.

"Sip together, the fruits of our labor," Soseki said. "What we start for all humanity, let the God of Winds finish. Bow and honor the noble kamikaze."

CHAPTER NINE

The muzzle of the old man's shotgun had been aimed skyward. Before the shotgun report died into the night, there was a second shot and the spotlight went dark. It was Carl with the Beretta.

"Don't shoot no more, Harold. Please, God, don't shoot. He's got a gun at my head, Harold," Jake screamed.

"Shut up, Jake," Harold yelled. "I'll get you out of there. Hold on."

"Listen to him, Harold. We don't want anyone hurt," Marc yelled, not really finding any comfort in knowing the old man's name now.

"Screw you, you slick city bastard," Harold yelled, and he fired the shotgun again.

"Give it up, Harold," Marc yelled as he maintained his deadly grip on Jake's neck, his previously wounded shoulder screaming with newly intensified pain. "You're empty and my partner is going to waste you if you try to reload."

"You can stick that idea up your brown-eyed ass," Harold yelled.

"Think it over, Harold. We just want to go on our way," Marc said. He had lost sight of Harold when Carl's shot put the light out. He knew the man was still in the same general vicinity, but he couldn't pinpoint him. He heard the breech of the double-barreled shotgun click open and the empties drop to the ground. In a couple of seconds, he heard the breech slam closed again.

"I'm comin' for your ass, boy. You boys is either poachers or you come to set fire to this here building. And around here, well, that's agin' the law," Harold yelled.

"Give it up, Harold. Don't cause old Jake to die," Marc said as he moved slowly toward the Cherokee for cover. It was insurance.

"Shit, boy, you're bluffin'. And besides that, old Jake knowed this job was dangerous when he took it," Harold said confidently.

"Come on, Harold, listen to this man. The sum-bitch got my own gun cocked up against my head. He ain't shittin', Harold. He's gonna kill me. Please, *please*, do what he says," Jake pleaded.

Marc heard footsteps. Harold was moving in his direction.

"Jake, don't go pissin' on yourself. I'll get you out of this," Harold said. "These bastards ain't that—"

Harold didn't have the opportunity to finish the sentence. Carl lunged from the shadows, a side kick stopping its momentum against Harold's testicles. Harold bowed over, the shotgun falling from his hands and his hands clasping his aching groin as he gasped for air.

Carl was up with a knee thrust just in time to meet Harold's face on the downturn. He heard bone break as his knee found Harold's nose. The big man fell to the ground amid gurgling sounds and vomit.

"He's down, brother. I got his weapons," Carl yelled.

Marc eased the revolver from Jake's head and tucked it into his waistband. He unsnapped a black leather case on the back of Jake's Sam Browne belt and pulled a pair of handcuffs from it. He took Jake's left arm first and cuffed the wrist. He slipped the free handcuff through Jake's trouser belt at the small of his back and then cuffed his right arm.

"What are you gonna do to us?" Jake asked nervously.

"We're not going to hurt you, if that's what you're asking. We just need to put you out of commission for a few hours." Marc prodded Jake forward toward Carl and Harold.

"I think this asshole would have killed us," Carl said when Marc and Jake stood beside him. He bent over the groaning old man and cuffed him with his handcuffs the same way Marc had cuffed Jake.

"Maybe." Marc surveyed the lighting arrangement for the spotlight at the edge of the pavement. What remained of the spotlight was sitting on a photographer's tripod with a car battery beside it on the ground. The entire arrangement was neatly covered with a lightweight camouflage tarp. "Let's give them a little something to make them sleep."

"I understand," Carl said, and he went to the Cherokee and retrieved his accessory bag. He drew a Mini Maglite from his pocket and found two needles and syringes.

Jake was horrified, his eyes open wide and full of fear in the ambient light of Carl's Mini mag. "You gonna kill us, ain't you? Oh shit, you're gonna kill us." Jake's voice was trembling and his body was shaking.

"Calm down," Marc said. "You're just going to take a little nap and when you wake up, you won't remember a thing. At the worst, you might have a hangover."

Carl rolled Jake's shirtsleeve up and wiped a small area with a disposable alcohol swab. He held the Mini mag between his teeth while Marc steadied Jake. He gave the trembling man the sedative injection and recapped the needle.

In three seconds, Jake collapsed into Marc's arms. He was sleeping soundly.

Harold was still moaning on the ground, his hands firmly cuffed behind his back. He tried to say something but his words were cut short when he threw up again. Carl unsheathed the second needle and injected Harold. It was a relief for the injured old lawman when the tranquilizing effects of the injection put him to sleep and masked the pain in his groin.

"Do it like Dallas?" Carl asked.

"Yeah, except leave their shirts and slip the belts from the trousers."

"What then?"

"They had to be driving something. You go look for it while I take their pants off."

Carl got his D-cell Maglite from the Cherokee and headed into the undergrowth behind the abandoned service station. In less than five minutes he returned.

Marc had removed the sleeping men's pants and put their belts back around their waists, with the handcuffs threaded through them in the back.

"There's a Chevy Blazer parked about a hundred yards back behind the building. A dirt road runs beside the building and directly to it," Carl said.

"Let's load them in the Cherokee and gather all their goodies. We'll lock them in the Blazer."

"Just want to leave them there?" asked Carl.

"Sure. By the time they wake up tomorrow, one way or another we'll be long gone." Marc started dragging Jake to the Cherokee.

"Yeah, old Harold is really going to be pissed when he wakes up without his pants," Carl said, and he laughed.

———

Mori Osamu stood silently in the shadows of a parked eighteen-wheeler. His all-black clothing caused him t blend with the darkness. The truckstop on the outskirts c Sacramento was extremely busy, with rigs cons' ntly driving in and out of the huge lot. Osamu waited for precisely the right rig, one that had just been refueled.

He spotted one coming from the fuel pumps. It was a white and red–painted White COE with a sleeper. The rig appeared relatively new, the paint still shiny rather than dull like rigs that had gathered some age. The trailer was a Fruehauf and it appeared to be older than the tractor. There was no lettering on the trailer and that would make the changeover more expedient. Aside from the required weights and permit numbers, there was no lettering on the tractor except the company name. It read, JACKSON TRANSIT— SPRINGFIELD, MISSOURI.

Osamu watched the driver carefully as he stopped the rig and left the engine running. The driver moved around for a few minutes inside the cab with the dome light on. He appeared to be doing paperwork. Several minutes passed and finally the door to the cab swung open. The driver, a man who looked no older than late thirties, climbed from the cab. The man was wearing a red plaid flannel shirt covered with a black leather vest. He wore western boots and jeans with a key holder on the belt. Osamu noticed the long leather wallet he carried in his back pocket. The wallet was attached to a small chain that terminated in a leather loop around his belt. Although Osamu was mentally cold and calculating, he almost smiled. He had always wondered what the drivers he had seen with similar wallets carried in them.

Osamu watched carefully until the driver disappeared inside the truckstop restaurant. The driver took a seat and a waitress sat a cup of coffee in front of him.

Osamu made his move, slipping through the shadows to the parked rig. He climbed up on the tractor and tugged on the door handle. It was locked. He quickly produced a spring steel lock pick from his shirt pocket and set to work on the door lock.

It took less than fifteen seconds to pick the lock. Osamu grabbed the handle again and opened the door.

The driver had left the rig running even after he departed for the restaurant and Osamu assumed he had two sets of keys. He had seen several drivers leave their rigs running and presumed the drivers' intent was to keep the engine at temperature and the cab comfortable. It was a serious error in judgment for the Jackson Transit driver.

Osamu ran a quick check of the instruments and everything appeared in order. The tanks were topped off, the gauges indicating full. The keys were in the ignition as an added convenience for the Friends of Humanity.

Osamu reached into the black Gore-Tex accessory bag strapped over his shoulder and came out with two large magnetic signs. He jumped from the rig and placed a sign on each door of the White COE tractor. In less than twenty seconds, JACKSON TRANSIT—SPRINGFIELD, MISSOURI, became COASTAL FREIGHTWAYS—SAN FRANCISCO.

The Japanese warrior moved quickly, his eyes constantly watching for any adversary. He saw none. He was back aboard the rig and shifting into gear before the Jackson Transit driver could sweeten his first cup of coffee.

Osamu left the truckstop and turned onto Interstate 5 North. He sailed through the gears until the rig was at highway speed and moving with the flow of traffic. He reached over and tested the BirdDog radar detector, which beeped and flashed an amber light, indicating it was working fine. He checked the CB, turned the volume up slightly, and verified it was on channel 19. Then he settled back into the airshock seat and enjoyed the ride.

The rig was nearly an hour out of Sacramento when Osamu heard a driver calling him on the CB.

"Hey, how 'bout you over there in that northbound White? What's it like over your shoulder?"

Osamu hesitated and then thought, why not? The more

natural he could act, the safer he would be. He picked up the microphone and spoke.

"This is that northbound White. It's lean and clean to the truckstop north of the Mento town," he said. His English was flawless; he hoped his CB jargon came across as well. His experience was limited to the time he had spent in this and one other stolen rig.

"Yeah, ten-roger on that. This is the Snatchbuster on this end. Who we got over there, come on?"

"Okay, Mister Snatchbuster, this is the Night Owl on this end. Where you headin'?" Osamu asked.

"Yeah, well, we be headin' to the Palm Beach town with the big hammer down. How 'bout you?"

"Goin' to Seattle and turnin' around," Osamu said into the microphone.

"Yeah, well, a ten-roger on Seattle. We be startin' to lose you, so have yourself a safe one out here on the superslab, Mister Night Owl. And remember, keep the big rig between the ditches and the little rig in your britches and you'll get back home alive. The Snatchbuster . . . we be gone. Bye."

"Thanks for the advice," Osamu said. "Have a good run." He placed the microphone back into its holder and stared out at the highway. Apparently he had faked it well, and the thought pleased him.

The big White ate the highway and digested the miles, leaving nothing but diesel smoke in the slipstream. Osamu concentrated on the white lines sliding by like savage spears as he drove on toward the salvation of mankind. In his mind, he had determined it was a most noble cause. The CB was filled with constant chatter echoing throughout the cab, but Osamu's full attention was focused on getting the rig to his final destination.

He didn't hear the movement in the sleeper bay or see the hand slip between the curtains.

———

"It is quite simple, really," Nagai Soseki said as he spoke to the two men who had received the noble honor of accomplishing the mission of death. "When you have found yourself void of all hope for completing your mission or reaching your destination, you simply press this black button. This is an activation switch for a ten-second time delay. Ten seconds from the time you press the switch, the cargo will detonate the explosive devices we have wired to the canisters. It will rain radiation for miles."

"It is an honor to pursue the salvation of all mankind, Honorable Soseki," said Natsume Shoyo.

He was the oldest of the chosen two, having lived for seventy-one years. The camp where he stood at this moment brought back memories and caused nightmares.

Shoyo had been in his late twenties when he and his young family were ordered by the United States government to abandon their home in San Francisco and were transported to a prison camp. He was told, at the time, that the encampment was for the safety of his family.

Shoyo went to the encampment willingly, trusting the promise given him by the government representatives. The encampment of safety turned into an entrenchment in hell. Two of Shoyo's children died within months, and soon his wife lost all touch with reality. She was released from the encampment for treatment in a mental institution. She died in that same institution twelve years later.

Shoyo never got over the needless deaths his family had suffered. Through his years of life, while he understood the reasoning of the government of the land of freedom, he never forgave the faceless bureaucrats. The honor he now found bestowed upon him was also an opportunity for vengeance. And it didn't matter to him that it came almost a half century too late.

"Will we detonate the canisters even if the government officials cooperate?" asked Danzai Yukio. Yukio was a student in the nuclear science program under Dr. Nagai Soseki. He was the youngest of the Friends of Humanity at age nineteen. His young age caused him to be no less dedicated to the cause of mankind's preservation.

Yukio's grandfather had died at Nagasaki when the American bomb came down. His father, then in childhood, suffered burns that scarred him for life. But it was not vengeance Yukio sought, it was preservation . . . preservation of life. And if it meant he had to kill thousands of people to preserve humanity, then his mission would be honorable.

"That will depend on the government officials and the electronic media," Soseki said with a sardonic grin. "We will do whatever is required to accomplish our ends."

"I understand," Yukio replied.

"We have forged the necessary paperwork for you to travel the highways. Danzai, I suggest you drive and Natsume can maintain an observant eye for potential interference," Soseki said.

"Very well," Yukio said. He showed signs of having consumed too much rice wine. His eyes were glazed and his balance slightly impaired by the alcohol.

"Come, and we shall indulge in one final sip of the nectar before you depart," Soseki said. "We should honor the noble men who will have the opportunity to push the button that will trigger a new age of awareness." He smiled at the chosen two, his deceptive face hiding reality.

What he hadn't told the honorable men was that the trigger mechanism also included a second timing device and a VHF receiver. The receiver was controlled by a phase-locked loop and microprocessor chip dedicated to one of the VORTAC aircraft navigational frequencies at Salt Lake City, Utah. When the receiver was within range of the navigation transmitter and locked on to its continuous-wave identifier, the timer would activate. The countdown to victory would be automatically initiated.

———

Carl was the first to reach the top of the rock pinnacle and slide out onto the giant outcropping on his stomach. Below him lay a canyon, concealed on three sides by high rock peaks. At first glance, the canyon appeared dark and void of habitation. Carl's heart sank momentarily as the thought occurred to him that they had miscalculated and disaster was imminent.

"See anything?" Marc asked in a soft whisper as he slid beside Carl on the outcropping.

"Yeah. Darkness," Carl replied. "We've blown it."

The statement had hardly left his mouth when the dark canyon filled with twin rays of white light. It seemed to emerge from the mountain itself like some medieval demon setting out on a rampage.

The dark silence filled with voices echoing off the canyon walls. Men were cheering wildly. And then there were flashlights and lanterns skipping along in the darkness behind the twin beams.

"What the—" Carl mumbled, the burst of activity taking him completely by surprise. He hoisted the infrared night vision binoculars to his face. He scanned the canyon and moved quickly from one focal point to another. "Holy shit!"

"What's going on down there?" asked Marc impatiently.

"Here, take a look for yourself," Carl said as he passed the binoculars to Marc.

Marc panned the canyon floor and made mental notes of the layout. He looked back against the mountain face and saw the huge entrance to a cave. He was bewildered. There were scores of men, all dressed in solid black, and their ages astounded him. There seemed to be no in-between; they were all either quite old or very young.

Marc laid the binoculars down, not believing what his eyes saw. "Looks like we hit the mother lode. I'll bet Harrison's right nut that that rig is loaded with nuclear waste."

"How many do you think are down there?" Carl asked.

"It looks like a small army. I think it's bigger than we thought. We can't go wading in there without support. It's too risky. Chances are, they have some plan for release of the toxic waste if they're attacked."

"We don't have time for backup. Even if we called in an air strike, that rig will be gone before anyone could get here," Carl said.

Marc looked through the binoculars again. He scanned the peaks surrounding the canyon encampment. "They have guards all around the canyon rim. I counted eight and there's probably more I didn't see."

"I don't see a lot of options," Carl said reluctantly.

"Me either," Marc replied. "We're going to have to let the rig get to the highway and hit it then. If we're lucky, they won't have communications with the camp or whoever is behind this. Maybe we can take them out before they reach their destination."

"Yeah, whatever it is. If they're hauling, we can't just blow the rig. We'll have to take the men and then get the goods."

"Any kind of heavy firepower could blow the canisters. This one's going to get touchy," Marc said.

"Damn, a silenced four-by-four all-terrain vehicle would sure be nice right now."

"Remember that." Marc stored the thought. It would be a good requisition for Harrison's people in Washington. "Since we don't have one, we'll have to hoof it back to the Cherokee. I don't want to lose that truck."

"They're not moving yet. You think they're moving all of the canisters?"

"I doubt it. Probably just enough to create mild havoc wherever they're going. If all of the canisters are down there, it would be too risky to move them all out at once. If they happened to get caught, they'd want some cards held in reserve."

"Make's sense," Carl said.

"Let's go take out the truck when it leaves. We can come back here and mop up the remains later. I'm anxious to see what's in that cave," Marc whispered as he started to get up from the rock outcropping.

Carl grabbed his arm and pulled him back down. "Listen. I heard something," Carl said in an excited whisper, and then he paused. "Over there, about thirty yards away—somebody's coming through the woods."

CHAPTER TEN

Mori Osamu heard the precision metallic clicks behind his head. There was no mistaking it—it was a revolver cocking. He froze and felt his heartbeat intensify. He had lost his usual edge of surprise and the table had abruptly turned.

Osamu was scared, so he didn't attempt to look behind him.

"Just keep both of your hands on the steering wheel and drive very deliberately to the shoulder of the road. Keep your eyes on the highway and don't try to look back. You mess up and I'll blow your eyes right through the windshield," said the woman who held the gun. Her voice was calm, with a cold tone lower than most women's. But more than anything else, her voice projected confidence.

Osamu kept his eyes on the highway and slowed the rig. Occasional headlights from oncoming traffic illuminated the inside of the rig from Osamu's left side. The light was adequate to cause a reflection of the cab's interior on the windshield. In the reflection, he could see a vague image of the woman. She had her head and her arms protruding through the sleeper curtain. The revolver was in her right hand. She had dark hair, either black or brown, but he couldn't tell which from the windshield image. He had to make a move, but he didn't know what just yet.

"I have to change gears or the rig will stall. I need to move my right hand," he said calmly.

"Bullshit," the woman said. "Push the clutch in and let it coast to a stop. You move those hands off the steering wheel and your ass is dead."

The woman was unmoving and Osamu realized he was going to die if he didn't do something. And if he died, then so might the vision of causing America to change its method of transporting nuclear death. He was overwhelmed with his own importance in the preservation of mankind. If he should die now, he knew the course of history might well go unchanged until it was too late for any logical pathway leading to salvation. The purpose of Friends of Humanity was far more important than the single life of some woman he had never seen before. In the course of the transition from one way of thinking to another, there would always be sacrifices. Osamu decided he wouldn't be one of them . . . not yet.

Traffic was light and consisted mostly of other eighteen-wheel rigs, with a few scattered cars. Osamu scanned the shoulder of the road as the rig slowed. Beyond the guardrail lay rugged terrain concealed in blackness. He decided to try to take the armed woman and then dispose of her body. The darkness and the terrain would make that job easier. But first he had to disarm her.

"You have some mighty tall explaining to do, mister," the woman said. "Where is Lou?"

"Who is Lou?" asked Osamu. He was playing dumb and stalling for time. He could develop a plan to escape, but he needed time and precisely the correct instant of opportunity. It hadn't come yet, but when it did the woman would die.

"Don't act so stupid. Lou Jackson is the man who was driving this rig when I went to sleep. He's also my husband. What did you do to him?" She was upset and her voice deepened.

"I left him sitting in the restaurant of a truckstop in Sacramento. He wasn't harmed."

"You damn well better hope he wasn't hurt. I ought to kill you anyway," the woman said as the rig slowly stopped on the shoulder of the highway.

"The rig is stopped. What will you do now—shoot me?" Osamu asked.

"That's up to you. Switch on the hazard flashers."

"Where's the switch?"

"On the master console beside the marker light switch. Move your left hand and keep your right hand on the steering wheel."

Osamu leaned cross-body and switched the hazard flashers on. He immediately put his left hand back on the steering wheel. The time to strike had not yet come.

"Now, with your right hand, open the door very slowly."

Osamu obeyed and the cab door opened into the night.

"Turn slowly to your left and climb from the cab. When you reach the ground, turn around facing away from the rig and walk out into the headlight beam. When you get there, go to the guardrail and lie down. If you move before I'm gone, I'll stop the rig and blow your head off. I can shoot a gnat off a groundhog's ass at fifty yards with this gun. If you don't think I can, just test your luck. Now get movin'," the woman said harshly.

"Are you just going to leave me on the side of the highway?" Osamu asked.

"You're lucky I'm not leaving you on the side of the highway with a bullet through your head. Now get movin' before I change my mind."

"That's not a very decent thing to do. All I wanted was a ride." Osamu was trying the pitiful approach and hoping he could appeal to the woman's conscience. If he could keep her talking, he could gain her confidence and then kill her.

"Bullshit!" the woman said. "You're just a sleazy thief. Now move!"

Osamu knew his immediate options were played out. He obeyed the gun-wielding woman and started from the cab. He climbed down carefully and consciously avoided anything that would cause the woman to squeeze the trigger. As his foot touched the pavement on the shoulder of the highway, his mind landed upon the plan.

Osamu was in the headlight beams when the woman finally climbed through the sleeper curtain. He kept walking and stood beside the guardrail. The woman slid into the driver's seat and grabbed the door. She slammed it closed and immediately locked it. She laid the revolver beside her right leg in the seat and reached for the gear shift.

Osamu watched the movement in the cab and then dropped into a prone position beside the guardrail just like the woman had told him to do. He heard the engine rev and watched as the rig slowly moved forward. He didn't move.

The rig inched forward and then the roar of the diesel engine was deafening as the woman floored the accelerator and slipped through the gears. In seconds, the rig was back on the highway and speeding off into the black of the night.

Osamu watched as the smoke trail from the rig's twin stacks faded into the darkness.

———

"He's coming this way," Marc said in a low whisper as he spread himself back out on the rock outcropping.

The footsteps were more audible now. The sound tore through the night. It was shoe leather scuffing against broken rocks and the rocks clacking against other rocks. The approaching human wasn't acclimated to the terrain and that meant he was probably a novice. If he was a novice, that could be good or it could be bad. A novice might not see the men stretched out on the rock outcropping, and that was good. The other side of the coin was bad: Even the slightest noise might spook him and cause him to open fire if he was armed. And there was little doubt in Marc's or Carl's mind that the man would be armed.

"Want to take him or let him pass?" Carl's voice was soft and low. It was barely audible even against Marc's ear.

"If he'll pass, let him pass. If he spots us, take him out," Marc replied in the same low voice.

The footsteps grew louder as the walker approached. He sounded like a person out for a casual midnight stroll. His steps were evenly paced and he made no effort to conceal his movements. He had cast away all caution, and that meant he felt secure. Marc and Carl suddenly felt the man was either a rank amateur or he had a death wish. If it was the latter, they could accommodate him.

The footsteps stopped. The man was twenty feet from the outcropping. He fumbled through his pockets and then the sound of wrinkling cellophane fell on the night. In a moment, there was a burst of light glowing yellowish orange. The man had struck a match and he held the fire to the tip of a cigarette. Marc and Carl could hear him breathe. It was a deep breath. The man held it for a moment, and then he exhaled. The smell of the cigarette smoke hung heavy on the crisp night air. It drifted over the outcropping and disappeared into the slow-moving air far above the canyon.

Marc could see the outline of the man clearly now. He stood against a tree with one leg propped up and the other one on the ground. An assault rifle of some type was draped across his left shoulder on a sling. He was leaning with his shoulders against the tree trunk, oblivious that the eyes of death were staring down on him. The cigarette hung casually in his hand and the burning tip was a glowing red-orange beacon in the night. Even in the darkness, the man was an easy target.

Marc and Carl waited. They were motionless on the giant flat rock that hung over the lip of the canyon. Seconds passed by and became minutes. The minutes seemed like hours as the man casually smoked his cigarette. Carl had the sights of his Beretta trained on the dark outline of the man's body. His hands were steady and his breathing was slowly deliberate. Marc lay outstretched with his Desert Eagle .357 Magnum automatic cocked and pointed at the man's head. He had used the point of the burning cigarette to determine where the doomed man's head was. When the burning cigarette was between his lips, hitting the man's head would be simpler than shooting out a streetlight.

More minutes passed and the distant sounds of the movement on the canyon floor intensified. Carl craned his neck slowly, glancing at the lights far below him. He could tell by the rolling sound echoing off the canyon walls as the diesel engine accelerated that the truck was beginning to move. If the guard stayed where he was, the truck could get away before Marc and Carl could get back to the Cherokee. If they hit the guard and simply hid his body, there could be big trouble before they could get back to the canyon after dealing with the rig. If the people below found the body or if the guard didn't return at all, it was a giant red flag. It would be very probable that the Delta Warriors could return to an empty encampment—or even worse, a death trap laid just for them.

Marc analyzed the situation carefully. At this particular moment, he would have gladly traded his Desert Eagle for a tranquilizer dart gun. He made a fast mental note to tell Harrison to get him one, but that wouldn't help now. Marc thought about the Parker-Imai survival knife strapped to his left leg. The knife would be quick and efficient, but more importantly, it would be silent. A single shot would send a report through the night for miles. Judging from the number of men he had seen on the canyon floor, it would be only minutes before the area above the canyon would be swarming with armed killers. And even if the guard fell from the shot, the rig would still get away.

Marc laid the Desert Eagle on the rock slowly and quietly. He reached to his left leg and silently unsnapped the retaining strap holding the giant knife. He positioned the knife in his right hand and started calculating his breathing. He judged the distance between where he was and his intented victim. If he moved skillfully, he could cover the twenty feet before the armed man could possibly react and make his weapon ready to fire. Killing the guard now wasn't his move of choice, but it was the only option he had.

Marc focused on the silhouette of a giant tree ten feet beyond the guard. He was carefully trying to avoid alerting any sixth sense the man might have that would warn him he was going to die. Marc counted off the seconds as he clutched the knife in his hand. It was poised and ready to end a human life. With the cunning of a cougar, Marc slowly came to his knees. He was ready to start the sprint toward his intended victim when a radio crackled and shattered the silence.

The guard dropped his cigarette to the ground and stamped it out with his boot. He fumbled for the radio on his hip and answered the call. Marc could hear the sound, but he couldn't understand what the conversation was about. In seconds, the guard was headed back the way he had come. It took less than a minute for the noise made by the man to vanish into the night.

"Let's hit it," Marc said. He was up and running before the words left his mouth.

Carl was behind him, following Marc's lead. It took several minutes for them to reach the Cherokee.

"If we hustle, we can get back to the rig and load before the truck winds its way out of the canyon. We've got to stop that truck," Marc said as he slammed the Cherokee into gear and headed for the overroad rig.

"I have a plan," Carl said, and he smiled as the Cherokee ripped through the night on the rough gravel road.

It was a race to save a nation.

———

"Sergeant, are you sure?" FBI Agent Ben Stacy said. The telephone had awakened him from a deep sleep. It was the first sleep he had been able to get since the whole affair started with the stolen nuclear waste materials. He sat up in his bed and his eyes opened wide. He couldn't believe what he was hearing. The caller had identified himself as Sergeant Todd Adams of the Los Angeles Police Department. He had unveiled the unfortunate scenario of Gary Merrill's fiery death.

"The license plate is registered to the FBI," Adams said. "That's all we have to go on right now."

"Are you sure the occupant was Agent Merrill?" Stacy asked.

"It may take weeks to be sure, but yes, we're sure. The body, or rather what remained of it, was in two pieces. It was severed about mid-chest. It was also burned beyond recognition. All we have to go on is the license plate on the car and an FBI badge found with the top part of the torso. There was also a model thirteen Smith & Wesson revolver in the vicinity of the lower torso. That's what you guys are issued. We'll run the serial number as soon as the lab boys can give us one. It was burned pretty badly," Adams said.

"Holy shit! Is there an indication of what might have happened? What I'm saying is, was it an accident?" Stacy asked.

"It looks that way. We have a statement from the driver of the truck. From what he had to say, they just didn't see each other until it was too late. He said he saw the red flashing light on the car just as it hit him."

"Has anyone notified his family?" Stacy hoped the answer was yes, but he knew it wouldn't be as soon as he asked the question.

"Oh no, you guys get that task," Adams said. His voice was melancholy and tinted with mild relief.

For a long moment, Stacy didn't speak. He sat there in nothing but his underwear and stared at the wall across the room. He knew he had just inherited the honors and he felt nauseated. He didn't know how he was going to tell Shirley that she was now a widow. "Okay, Sergeant, we'll handle it." Stacy hoped the sick feeling inside his stomach didn't carry over to his voice. It wouldn't be professional to do that because it might embarrass the bureau. And with Gary Merrill's death and the death of the banker from Little Rock, the bureau didn't need any more embarrassment.

"I don't envy you," Sergeant Adams said. "If we find anything else, I'll call you."

"Thank you, Sergeant," Ben Stacy said, and he laid the telephone handset back into its cradle. He laid back down in his bed and stared blankly at the ceiling. Several moments passed and his mind kept returning to the same thought. He kept wondering what Merrill had found that would have caused him to be running an emergency in a direction out of L.A. Stacy knew that whatever it was, it must have been extremely important. Unless his mind was completely preoccupied, there was no way Merrill would have missed seeing a tractor-trailer coming into an intersection. He was too good at what he did to make a mistake like that.

Stacy got up from the bed and put his pants on. After he told Shirley the tragic news, he had to find out what Merrill knew that had cost him his life.

———

Jill Lanier scanned through the magazine as she sat in bed. The flight to Washington, D.C., had been tiring, but she had found herself unable to go to sleep. The magazine was simply a distraction from her thoughts . . . from her concern for Marc.

There was a light knock at the door. Jill laid the magazine aside and walked to the door after pulling on the only nightcoat she had brought with her. She peeped through the security viewfinder and saw Brittin Crain standing in the hallway.

"Were you sleeping?" Crain asked when Jill opened the door.

"No, I was reading a magazine. I'm tired but I can't seem to go to sleep," Jill said as she stepped back and invited Crain inside.

"Me either," said Crain softly. "You're worried about Marc, aren't you?"

"Sure. You know, Brittin, I had my life pretty much together until Marc came back to Texas. And then everything went haywire. Leeco and my job there had been my life. . . . I guess I'm not making any sense, am I?"

"If it makes you feel better, keep talking," Crain replied as he made himself at home and slumped into one of the armchairs in a corner of the room.

"Well, I guess what I'm saying is I don't understand what is happening here. You told me Marc and Carl were arrested by the FBI and now they're on some crazy damned secret mission. It all sounds like a fairy tale. No, it sounds like a bunch of bullshit," Jill said angrily.

"You've been through a lot these last few weeks. And you know, Jill, whether you understand it or not, you've shown you have a lot of spunk. We're all heading into something that may be bigger than any of us realizes. Do you consider yourself patriotic?"

"Yes, well, I suppose so. What does that have to do with anything?" asked Jill testily.

"It has everything to do with it. People like Marc, Carl, you, and me . . . well, it's people like us who can make a difference."

"You're about as clear as concrete. Say it without going around in circles. What is it with you men, anyway? You sound just like Marc. Can't you guys ever give a concise answer about anything?"

"Okay, I'm sorry. Let me try again. What this is all about is developing your spunk, channeling your energy, and taxing your mind with new skills until they become second nature. All of the death and destruction we've all seen in the last few weeks hasn't been without purpose. It's caused a profound change that affects all four of us. So much has changed, in fact, that none of us can ever go back to the way it was."

"Why? Why can't we try? Life wasn't this complicated two months ago."

"We can't go back because what we knew two months ago doesn't exist anymore. There's a place for you in all this. Marc saw to it. We're all in the middle of major changes and when they're finished, we're going to stomp the shit out of the criminal maniacs in this country," Crain said. His lips were tight and his face became hard. His jaw jutted and stretched his facial skin as he clenched his teeth.

"You mean we're all going to be vigilantes?"

"No!" Crain said emphatically. "Not vigilantes. You and

I will be part of a sophisticated support team. Marc and Carl are the point men. What we do has been sanctioned. We're going to start sweeping up some of the sacks of shit that are polluting this nation and kick ass one crime at a time."

CHAPTER ELEVEN

The wind drag was punishing. Mori Osamu forced his muscles to function. He abruptly realized he had spent too many hours behind a desk and too few hours in the gym. He struggled to maintain his grip on the axle of the giant eighteen-wheel rig. He held tightly to the rusted steel shaft as the highway flashed by him only inches from his head. He finally managed to move enough to stretch his arm upward to one of the twin steel beams supporting the fifth wheel on the rear of the White tractor. His fingers could touch the cold steel but he couldn't move enough to secure his grip without losing his hold on the axle. He knew that if he slipped, eighty thousand pounds of rig and cargo would make minced hamburger out of his body. And if that should happen, the purpose would be lost.

For the first time since he made his emergency plan and then implemented it, Osamu wondered if perhaps he should have taken his chances with the revolver that had been pointed at his head. The roar of the engine was deafening beneath the rig as it streaked north on Interstate 5. The plan had seemed practical at the time he had made the decision. And until now, implementation had been simple. He had waited for the rig to move out along the shoulder of the highway. As the unsuspecting woman who drove the rig shifted through the gears and tried to build speed, Osamu had simply jogged along beside it. He was careful to stay out of the rearview mirror's field of view. At precisely the most opportune instant, he had jumped under the moving rig and grabbed the axle. But now, what Osamu had considered genius had become a potentially fatal nightmare.

Osamu strained as the rig roared along the dark highway. Every muscle in his body screamed from overexertion. But this time, his fingers made the connection with the steel beam and wrapped around it. His body was depleted of energy and he operated solely on adrenaline. He reached deep within his soul and found a new burst of strength to raise his body from the grips of the grim reaper. Sheer will and adrenaline reigned, and gradually his body moved from the perch of death beneath the rig.

In a surge of rage and defiance of the prospects of his body becoming ground dead meat, Osamu ascended through the steel structure of the White diesel tractor. The seconds it took to make the climb felt like an eternity, but soon he sprawled on the steel beams in front of the fifth wheel. He stared up at the bottom of the trailer's front lip and the ugly aluminum frame was suddenly a dazzling thing of beauty to his eyes.

Osamu stayed in the same position for several minutes until his breathing and heartbeat returned to normal. He smiled at himself for having cheated death out of a victory party. It was his turn to celebrate now, and he decided to start the festivities by taking back the rig he had been evicted from. And this time, revolver or no revolver, the bitch would die.

Osamu stood slowly and fought the wind drag for his balance on the steel beams. The area behind the cab seemed trapped in a vacuum that pressed him forward against the cab. The slipstream of invisible air sailed by on each side of the rig at better than sixty miles per hour. It was time for the death dance again, and any slip, any mistake, would plummet the purpose into dismal failure. It was a heavy burden, in addition to his own survival, but it was one he accepted as a challenge. He would survive and the purpose would be fulfilled. It was the way of the Japanese warrior to survive.

Traffic was sparse. Only one other rig had passed them since Osamu had made his daring attempt to capture the rig. He stayed down in the shadow of the trailer when the big brown commercial carrier came alongside. Once it was past, he breathed a sigh of extreme relief. If he were spotted on the back of the rig, it could spell instant disaster. He glanced to the rear of the trailer and looked for headlights. He saw none and he felt revived.

Osamu assumed the California Highway Patrol had already been notified of the rig's disappearance. It would take time for an officer to get to the truckstop and even more time for the report to be filed. And even if CHP was looking for Jackson Transit's White diesel, they wouldn't find it. If the rig were suspicious for some reasons, it still bore the name of Coastal Freightways. It was a calculated risk that the stranded driver carried no record of his identification numbers or license plate numbers. It would require hours to get in contact with his dispatcher and trace the proper numbers. And in the time it took them to complete the trace, the rig would undergo sufficient transformation to make identification all but impossible.

The wind flow threatened his footing as Osamu slipped his hand onto the side of the rig. The rig had been given a coat of wax recently and his hands slipped without resistance over the glossy surface. The slick surface made Osamu's movement more treacherous. All it would take would be a slight miscalculation and he could lose his balance. If he fell now, he would tumble into either the four tires on the driver's side or beneath the trailer. Neither fall left any margin for his personal survival. He moved slowly with the cunning of a big cat and the dexterity of a snake as he slithered closer to his intended victim. He hugged the framework of the big cab, his body spanned out against the back of it like a waffle on a plate.

Osamu suspected the woman who controlled the rig would look for the first exit from the superhighway. If he had predicted accurately, she would take the exit and reenter the highway on the other side. She would then go back to Sacramento and check every truckstop until she found the one where the man she had identified as her husband was abandoned. He knew he had to make his move before the rig reached the exit.

Osamu looked behind the rig for traffic that might be approaching. The only thing he saw was a pair of headlights more than a mile behind them. He reached around the side of the rig with his left hand and found the climbing handrail beside the driver's door. He glanced at the rearview mirror. The woman was busy watching in front of her. So far, she hadn't looked into the left mirror. It was a strain to touch the handrail, but he made it. The wind at sixty miles per hour was torturous and it slapped at his body with unrelenting force. Once his fingers were wrapped around the railing, he was ready to move. A final thought shot through his mind like a bolt of lightning, and for an instant he felt nauseous. He hoped the woman hadn't locked the door.

The assailant gripped the climbing rail with every ounce of strength in his body. His heart pumped at a brutal rate and sent a rush of adrenaline crashing through his veins. He swung around, clutching the rail, and suddenly he was swinging freely against the side of the rig. His hand slipped down the railing, gliding without resistance down the smooth chrome surface. The air crashed into him and almost took his breath away. He gasped and squeezed tighter on the rail. It didn't work. His hand still slid on the chrome bar. Then there was a flash of pain. His hand was burning from the friction. He gritted his teeth and kicked softly at the side of the rig. He looked down. His feet were almost touching the pavement. He knew that even with a slight encounter with the road surface he would lose some toes. And if the impact came abruptly enough, he could lose a foot. But that wasn't the worst of it. Even just touching the road surface would surely dislodge his hand-grip, and he would fall to his death a dismal failure.

Osamu reached inside his soul again and found a new birth of strength. The wind continued to batter him and the cool night air slamming into him at sixty miles per hour caused him to shiver. He realized he was sweating, and a chill caused by the air ravaged his moist body. It was the new strength given only from his soul that saved him from the clinging arms of eternity. He moved his legs forward and the tip of his toes touched on an island of refuge. He had found the footstep on the side of the cab.

With the grace of a trained fighter, Osamu brought his other hand to the railing and stabilized himself. He had neither seen nor felt any indication the woman driver had spotted him. But even if she had, he was beyond the threshold of return and he would accomplish his mission or die trying.

He stepped on the step now with both feet. He kept one hand on the railing and reached for the door handle with his left hand as he fought the wind drag. The sheer forces of nature tore at him and tried to pluck him from his perch, but he held on. A strange sensation smothered his body and soothed his soul. From some unknown origin and clothed in a strange mystical peace, he felt the great scythe of the grim reaper start in motion toward his heart.

He tugged on the flat chrome door handle. It didn't move.

———

Marc slammed the last door closed on the trailer. He tucked the lock in his pocket. He heard the rig idling as dark smoke chugged from its twin chrome stacks and disappeared into the starlit night. He secured the latch handle and put the lock in his pocket. An Uzi submachine gun swung freely on its sling from his right shoulder. He had driven the Cherokee into the trailer and loaded the ramps while Carl warmed the rig. The big diesel was almost at temperature, and not a moment too soon. He heard the sounds of another diesel approaching from the direction of the encampment. There was no doubt in his mind that it was the load of stolen nuclear waste.

Marc ran along the side of the rig until he reached the cab door. He opened it and then climbed in, snapping the Uzi from his shoulder and laying it in his lap. "They're coming."

"I'm ready when they are." Carl had already put the rig in gear and his left foot kept the clutch depressed. He had his right foot on the accelerator, waiting for the truckload of death to emerge from the darkness.

The wait was short. Headlights came from the darkened mountain silhouettes and illuminated the narrow road in front of him. The light preceded the roar of the engine as the rig finally took shape against the darkness. In the time it took Carl to ease out the clutch, the rig passed by the Delta Warriors. In the ambient light of the rig's headlights, Marc and Carl read the company name on the cab door at almost the same time. It was a Coastal Freightways truck.

Carl stepped hard on the accelerator and the big rig lurched to life. At first it jerked forward as Carl slipped through the gears. He built up speed and finally saw the taillights of the Coastal rig as both highway machines approached the entry ramp to Interstate 5.

"Keep them in sight, but don't get too close. We don't want to spook them," Marc said.

"Roger, Colonel. How long you want to let them roll before we hit 'em?"

"Long enough to get away from this general area. We don't know what kind of communications equipment they have and we certainly don't want the reinforcements back at the camp to come running."

"Or worse yet, we don't want them to blow the other canisters if they still have some back at the canyon," Carl added.

"Could you tell anything about the occupants when the rig passed?"

"I couldn't see shit except the name on the side of the door."

"Me either."

The outlaw rig turned onto the ramp and headed south. Carl followed without speaking. Both rigs rolled up to highway speed and streaked through the night toward Sacramento.

"You think they're going to L.A.?" asked Carl, finally breaking the silence.

"It's anybody's guess. It's their ball game. All we can do is tag along until our guts tell us it's time to strike."

"You know if they're carrying that nuclear shit they're going to have it booby trapped. You think we should call in some support?"

"No, my feeling is still the same. The fewer people who know about this, the smaller the risk of someone screwing it all up," Marc replied. "The wheels of bureaucracy have a tendency to do that sometimes."

Carl steered the rig through the night. He followed the overroad rig from the encampment, carefully keeping a safe distance so the driver wouldn't become suspicious. "It's less populated in this area than it is around Sacramento. I think we need to hit them before they get to an area where a leaky canister could do extensive damage."

"I'm for that," Marc said. "We'll call Harrison by radio tomorrow morning if we don't have this thing wrapped up by then. He's probably off somewhere in dreamland right now."

"If we could take these people alive, it might give us some answers."

"I agree. We need to know how involved this thing is. I suspect the tentacles run deeper than we know. It's too complicated for a group of simpletons to pull off. These people had to have access to scheduling, routing, and God knows what else to know when and where to hit. Whoever these people are, they know what they're doing."

"You saw the bodies running around back there in the canyon. That's a lot of trigger fingers. If there are that many people at the encampment, how many more are there out here that we don't even know about?" Carl added.

"Someone in a place of importance had to know what to hit . . . what would be the most devastating if they had to follow through with their threats. What bothers me most is that the first deadline has come and gone and we haven't heard a word from them."

"Yeah, but that rig is sure rolling in front of us. Maybe that's their next calling card," Carl said. "This isn't like a hit with Delta Force. At least when we went in somewhere, we already had the enemy identified. We don't know who or what we're dealing with here. This is some spooky stuff, man."

"I second that. Think what might have happened if old Jake and Harold had run across the encampment."

"Yeah, they could have helped with population control. They'd have gone in there like a herd of elephants."

"They would have gotten their asses shot off, that's what would, have happened. I'm glad you remembered the sedatives. Those two guys are probably sleeping better in the back of that Blazer than they've slept in years. They'll never know how they got there," Marc said, laughing.

"It's funny now, but it wasn't too funny when it happened," Carl added, and he wasn't laughing.

"Ease on up beside these guys and let's see what we can see," Marc said.

Carl increased his speed and gained on the outlaw rig. The Caterpillar diesel whined under the hood as pure horsepower transferred to the drive shaft and ended where the rubber met with the pavement. The highway was void of other traffic except a few rigs running northbound. In less than a minute, he was beside the outlaws. The unmarked rig Carl drove was in the left passing lane and the outlaw rig drove precisely at the speed limit in the right lane. Marc looked over to the driver of the Coastal Freightways rig and shot him a friendly wave.

The young driver waved back and smiled.

Marc reached for his CB microphone with his left hand. He gripped the pistol grip of the Uzi in his right after he flicked off the safety. "Top of the evenin' to you, Mister Coastal Freightways. Who we got over there?"

The young driver hesitated, but then reached for his microphone. "This is Chop Stick over here, go ahead."

"Okay, Mister Chop Stick. Say, let's drop down to channel thirteen. I want to ask you something of a personal nature," Marc said, playing the CB role for all it was worth.

"Go on," the driver replied.

Marc leaned over to the CB and switched to channel 13. He pressed the switch to talk. "Mister Chop Stick, are you here?"

"I'm here, go ahead," the driver replied.

"What the hell are you going to do?" Carl asked testily.

"Watch," was Marc's only reply. He looked at the driver as Carl kept the rigs side by side. "Pardon me, Mister Chop tick, but would you happen to have any stolen nuclear waste on board?"

"Shit, man!" Carl yelled. "What the hell are you doing?"

"It's called the direct approach," Marc replied. He could see the stunned driver drop his microphone. He turned toward Marc and shot him a panic-stricken look. The next thing Marc saw was a bright flash licking from the barrel of a pistol. The driver's window in the Coastal rig shattered and fell onto the highway. The pistol bullet harmlessly struck the door below Marc's knees.

Marc was up with the Uzi. He quickly rolled his window down and returned fire. The rattle of the subgun spit sizzling 9mm death at the Coastal rig and filled the cab of his own rig with ear-splitting reverberations.

The driver panicked. He had been caught totally off guard. He floored the accelerator and the Coastal rig leapt ahead as the diesel engine churned thick black smoke from the stacks.

Carl reacted. He stomped his own accelerator and brought the rig up to the rear wheels of the Coastal tractor. The driver was steering with one hand and firing wildly with the other. Bullets slammed into the windshield just over Carl's head and flew harmlessly into the headliner of the cab. The big warrior remained calm.

"Take it up two more feet," Marc shouted.

The Peterbilt moved forward, both rigs dangerously gaining speed. Marc leaned from the window and fired the Uzi with bursts of flames licking into the night. The flying death pellets found their mark in the cowling of the outlaw rig. In seconds, there was a geyser of steam gyrating from the front of the outlaw tractor.

Marc changed sticks in the Uzi and slammed a full one up the well. He felt it seat and gripped the charging lever. Then he slapped it back in a quick motion and let it slam closed. In the same motion, he grabbed the pistol grip with

his right hand and moved the Uzi out of the window. He
fingered the trigger and lit the night with hellfire. The
terrorist driver fought for control but Marc's projectile
perforated his front tires.

The outlaw rig swerved first left and then right as the
driver battled the steering wheel. Marc was firing again
the Uzi sending flying death into the cab. More shots came
from the outlaw rig, but this time they were coming from in
front of the driver's face. It was the passenger firing an
automatic weapon at Marc and Carl.

Carl swerved and the trailer screamed behind him from
the abrupt maneuver. The rig rocked and threatened to
fishtail. Carl compensated and corrected the wild movement.

The terrorist driver was out of control. The radiator
steam was almost blinding him. A slick layer of water
and antifreeze coated the windshield. When the driver
switched on his wipers, he found only a severed wiper arm
scraping against the glass; one of Marc's bullets had blown
the wiper away.

The outlaw rig veered sporadically and flew from one
side of the highway to the other. Carl dropped back and let
the outlaw rig take the lead again. Marc unleashed a final
burst and fired out the stick. The bullets hammered into
the outlaw rig with devasting effectiveness. The rearview
mirror disappeared and a severed CB antenna plummeted
to the highway. In a final death throe, the outlaw rig
slithered like a snake, jackknifed, and careened through the
guardrail.

CHAPTER TWELVE

Mori Osamu struggled to keep his grip on the handrail and maintain his balance on the metal step of the speeding overroad rig. The wind slapped his face with unyielding force and punished him as the rig continued north on Interstate 5. He reached into his pocket and his fingers sought the touch of slender cold spring steel. He found the lock picks and slipped one from his pocket. Reaching up to the door lock, he inserted the curving end of the small black spring steel shaft into the metal lock housing.

The rig shifted momentum and slowed. Osamu dropped down as far as he dared and strained the muscles in his arms as he held tightly to the railing. He looked up to the driver's window. The woman driving the rig still had her attention focused on the highway. Osamu looked to his left across the median to the southbound lane of the interstate highway. An overroad rig sat in the middle of the highway. It had its hazard flashers blinking a warning into the night. Another rig was jackknifed into the guardrail.

There was a sudden lurch and the whine of the diesel engine intensified as the driver moved back up to normal speed. The wreck scene disappeared into the night. Osamu felt his grip loosening and he found it strange that he was sweating in the cool night temperatures. He attributed the perspiration to exertion because he had closed his mind to fear. He jiggled the lock pick and tried to make the lock open, then looked back up at the driver. It was then he realized picking the lock wouldn't be necessary . . . he was staring into the barrel of a revolver.

Glass shards slammed into his face in the same instant he saw the deadly flash. The impact jolted him and slapped him away from the door. He was swinging over the white lines on the highway, his body flapping in the breeze like the tail of a kite. He dropped the tiny lock pick and forced his left hand to move to the railing. He kicked against the wind force and found his perch again.

Another shot rang into the night, the bullet missing its intended mark. The safety glass from the window completely disintegrated and showered the assailant with cutting missiles. Osamu reacted out of instinct. He threw his left hand to the window and grabbed for the weapon. His aggressive movement was answered by still another gunshot. He felt a stinging pain burning his arm. He jerked it back quickly and saw the course of a bullet that had grazed his arm and left a superficial wound. He knotted his fist and the pain temporarily subsided as blood oozed from the wound. It was only then that he felt the warmth from the blood trickling down his face. The glass had lacerated his face in a dozen places like low-velocity shrapnel.

The woman was smart and she was also good. She drove with her left hand and fired with her right. She kept her head swiveling from the highway to Osamu and back again. The rig held steady on its course and was unaffected by the fracas.

Osamu felt his body failing as fatigue took its toll. He looked deep into his soul, into the purpose of his mission, and found another burst of inner strength. He ignored the searing pain in his arm and the multiple lacerations on his face. He thanked the gods that the glass fragments had missed his eyes. He knew it was only by the spiritual blessings of his mission's purpose that he had retained his eyesight. And if he could see the crazy bitch, he could kill her.

He coiled his fist tightly and held his thumb firmly into his fingers. He raised the fist over his head in a movement that simulated a high block, then let out a heart-stopping scream and leapt for the space where the window once was. His body slammed into the side of the rig as his fist sailed through. For an instant he thought his hand had left the railing, but he squeezed even harder and maintained his grip.

The impact was devastating. Osamu's fist crashed into the side of the driver's head with brutal force. She was stunned, but she kept control of the rig. Tiny bursts of starlight shot through her eyes like the hot glowing droppings of a Fourth of July sparkler. Blood quickly seeped from a laceration on her scalp. She thought she was going to black out when the starlights faded. She struggled with the steering wheel to keep the rig on the road, though she had let off the accelerator for a second when the impact of the fist knocked her sideways in her seat.

The lights stopped swirling in her head and the blackness was replaced with headlights glaring down the super highway. Janie Jackson returned the brutal force thrust at her with like kind, firing out the revolver. When Osamu's hand came through the window again, she beat it with the barrel of the gun. But it wasn't enough. Osamu's hand slammed into her head again and again. The headlights faded and the starlights swirled more rapidly. Janie felt the blood flowing from her head now. It had run down her face and neck, soaking her shirt. The revolver fell from her limp fingers when the final blow from the skilled assailant thrust her from the driver's seat.

Osamu climbed to the door. He reached inside through the open window and unlocked it. For the first time, Osamu saw the name "Janie" embroidered above her breast pocket. The rig swerved and slowed slightly, but it managed to stay on the highway. Osamu opened the door and climbed in as the rig ate the blacktop at over fifty miles per hours. He shoved the unconscious body of Janie Jackson from the driver's seat and into the passenger area, then quickly took control of the rig and settled into the seat.

The revolver was on the floorboard at his feet. It was empty and useless, but Osamu didn't need it anyway. He kicked it under the seat frame and out of the way of his feet. He looked at the trail of blood left by the courageous woman, then reached to his arm again and touched the burning wound inflicted by the woman's bullet. He immediately scanned the rearview mirrors to check on the flow of traffic behind him. A sadistic smile crept to his face when he saw the only headlights following him were still at least a mile away.

Osamu reached over to Janie's unconscious body and grabbed her by the belt. He pulled steadily until she was sitting upright in the passenger seat. Her head sagged against her chest as blood flowed from the wounds made by his hands. He leaned hard to the right, across her bloody form, and unlocked the passenger door. Then he pulled the handle and the door moved freely. It wouldn't open all the way because the wind drag forced it closed.

The angry attacker pushed against Janie until she was against the door. When he had her body in the right position, he gave a mighty shove.

"Good-bye, bitch!" Osamu said, and he shrieked a sadistic laugh. "You should have learned to use that gun just a little better."

Janie Jackson tumbled from the cab, and Osamu felt a slight shudder throughout the rig as the speeding tires rolled over her.

———

Ben Stacy wasn't sure what he was looking for, but he hoped if he found it he would recognize it. He sat at Gary Merrill's desk at the FBI office in Los Angeles. He felt strange. It was an eerie feeling he couldn't explain. It had only been a few hours since Merrill sat at the same desk, and Stacy felt it was here that Merrill had found the link or the clue that had cost him his life. He hoped that, through some serious investigation and a little luck, he could find what it was Gary Merrill had placed enough importance on to lose his life.

It had been one of the worst things he had ever done when he drove across town to Shirley Merrill's house. It was the sludge detail . . . telling someone that their spouse or loved one wasn't coming home again. And when that loved one was an agent, a fellow lawman, it made it even tougher.

Stacy had hoped Shirley would be strong. He had mumbled a prayer on the drive to her house. It was a simple request to whatever power there might be beyond the visibility of man's recognition. He had known before he rang the doorbell what her reaction would be. He had known that as soon as she saw him the butterflies would start in her stomach. There would be the initial shock and then the hysterics. After the crying, there would come the one solitary question no one could ever answer. Why?

Shirley had played the scenario just as Ben expected she would. She was a strong woman, a strong wife. But she wasn't *that* strong. Ben had spent some time with the newly widowed woman. He waited until a few friends and then some relatives from her side of the family had come to the house. At the first respectable opportunity, he had given his condolences and left.

He thought about Gary and Shirley Merrill. And then there were the kids—that was an entirely different heartbreak. Shirley and Gary both knew it could always happen. But Gary, like most every person who wears a badge and carries a gun, always denied it. It could never happen to him, or at least he always told himself that. All cops do. It was something people with a badge were never taught in training: how to die gracefully. Merrill knew and Stacy knew it was much easier to face death when you didn't think it could happen or you didn't know it was coming. The psychotherapy types called it denial, but the people who lived every day in the shadow of death called it survival methodology.

Stacy moved the clutter of paperwork around on Merrill's desk. Maybe, just maybe, the clue was there. If it wasn't, maybe something was there that would cause the pieces to come together. Stacy looked through the stack of reports from the other field agents. He scanned one after another, but nothing triggered anything abnormal.

He removed a rubber band from a stack of files labeled only "Terrorists." He looked at the notations under the rubber band on a scrap of paper and found that most of the files were from the late sixties and early seventies. The files represented known Asian radical groups and activists who were involved in violent antiwar and antigovernment activities during the Vietnam War era. The files were in no particular sequence, so Stacy started to flip through them: Communist Chinese–supported cells, Red Army affiliates, Japanese terrorists of all stripes—far right and far left.

Fifteen minutes passed and the clue still hadn't surfaced. Ben thought perhaps the clue, the single strategic link, died in the flaming wreckage with Gary Merrill. The activist stack had worn down and Stacy picked up another folder. He opened it and saw a man standing in front of a college campus sign. He was holding a picket sign that said, NO NUKES. The man was younger, his hair much longer, but the face seemed to jump from the file folder and assault

Stacy's mind. Even with the change in the hair and the difference in the age, there was no doubt in Stacy's mind it was the same man.

He flipped back to the first page of the folder. The name on the file didn't match the name Stacy knew. The folder indicated the man in the picture was a Japanese-born radical named Mori Osamu. He had been a nuclear and environmental science major at the University of California, Davis campus. His arrest sheet indicated he had been arrested with a college professor named Nagai Soseki for unlawful demonstrations in 1969. The demonstrations had been sponsored by antiwar and antinuclear groups during the height of the Vietnam War.

Ben Stacy held the folder in his left hand and reached for the telephone with his right. He dialed a three-digit number and waited.

"Communications," the answering voice said.

"Freddie, this is Ben Stacy. Can you patch me through to Mr. Lee and Mr. Browne on the Department of Defense national repeater system?"

"Yeah, it may take a couple of minutes. Can I call you back?" Freddie replied.

"Sure, I'm at Gary Merrill's extention. Make it quick, all right?"

"Got it. Hey, sorry to hear about Gary. It's a damn shame."

"I know," Stacy said. "You just get that call through and maybe we can wrap this thing up for Gary. We owe him one."

"You bet!" The line cleared.

Stacy stared at the face in the color photograph. Osamu was smiling as if he were very proud of what he was doing. Sure, time had changed some features about the man, there was no doubt about that. But there was one thing time wouldn't change, and Stacy would recognize that gold incisor anywhere.

———

Marc hit the pavement before Carl had the rig completely stopped. He was beside the outlaw rig and reaching for the door handle before the two men inside could gather their senses. Both were bleeding extensively from lacerations inflicted by the impact. Although only semiconscious, they were moving inside the rig. The door was jammed from the crash but Marc finally jerked it open.

There was a blinding flash and a deafening roar. Marc was met at the open cab door with rapid gunfire. It was the young driver thrusting a handgun through the opening and firing like a wild maniac. The shots missed and Marc fell back, hugging the pavement at the side of the rig.

Carl had managed to stop the huge eighteen-wheeler in the middle of the superhighway. He switched on the hazard flashers and bolted from the rig, taking cover at the right front fender of his own cab.

More shots rang out into the night. Carl spotted Marc lying at the edge of the outlaw trailer. The rig was leaning precariously, perched on nothing but air and what remained of a guardrail. Marc motioned Carl to the rear of the trailer. Carl darted around the blind side of his own rig and sprinted for the outlaw trailer through the clear area of thirty feet that separated the rigs on the highway.

There was more gunfire, and this time it was the slow cyclic sound of a Thompson submachine gun. The Thompson rattled .45-caliber death into the nothingness of the night. But the hot hardballs slammed harmlessly into the pavement and richocheted into the darkness, missing any target by at least several yards.

Marc held his fire, securing his position of safety beneath the tilting trailer. He wanted the outlaws alive . . . if possible. The only way the occupants of the cab could possibly fire at him with any degree of certainty would be to either climb from the cab or lean into a clear fire field. Either way they went, it would be deadly for them and Marc would be a tough target to hit from his position on the ground.

More gunfire disrupted the night. It was a double tap from Carl's Beretta at the rear of the trailer. In seconds, Marc heard the metallic squeak as the doors begrudgingly swung open behind him. Marc could hear fast footsteps above him, inside the trailer. The running stopped abruptly.

"Oh, shit!" Carl yelled, and the footsteps disappeared toward the back of the trailer.

Traffic was stalled on the highway now. Cars, light trucks, and overroad rigs were blocking the highway. The few brave souls who had ventured toward the jackknifed rig became hidden from view when gunfire broke the silence. So far there had been no sirens, and Marc thought that was good. He remembered what the president had said about hitting hard and fast and disappearing before anyone of authority could get to the scene. The terrorists in the front of the rig didn't make it easy for the president's plan to work smoothly. But, Marc thought, even the gears of justice needed a little grease now and then.

Danzai Yukio bolted from the cab door with the muzzle of his pistol spitting smokeless death. Dirt and chips of pavement splintered into Marc's face. Marc threw his arm over his eyes, shielding them from the gritty spray. He still held his fire as the crazed shooter ran into the gap between the two rigs and stopped.

"Shoot me, American pigs, and I will detonate the canisters where they lay," Yukio said as blood flowed freely down his face. He was unsteady on his feet and trembling.

He held a black box about the size of a pack of cigarettes in his left hand and the pistol in his right.

Marc leveled his sights on the man's chest and eased the trigger back slightly. He paused, deliberately controlled his breathing, and held the shot. He looked carefully at the box that was now clearly visible in the headlights glaring down on the young man. There was a shiny telescopic antenna protruding from the top of the box. The man held it sideways and Marc could see a couple of pushbutton switches and a glowing green light-emitting diode.

Marc immediately knew why Carl had cursed and left the trailer so quickly. He also knew he was lying in a very bad place. If the maniac pushed the button, Marc knew he would have the honor of being the first to go, if only by a few microseconds.

"There is no escape for you. Put the box down and surrender," Marc pleaded. "We will not harm you."

Yukio screamed, "You have already harmed me. You and your kind have harmed all mankind with your nuclear experiments and the proliferation of radiation as a way of life. It is a way of death." He tightened the grip on he detonator transmitter.

"Who are you?" asked Marc coldly.

"I am a dedicated soldier for the Friends of Humanity."

"You have a name?"

"I am called Danzai Yukio."

"Danzai, do you want to die tonight?"

"I do not fear death. It is my mission to die for the purpose of mankind's salvation," Yukio said nervously.

"What is it you and your people seek?"

"We demand the cessation of careless transportation of nuclear materials across the highways of this country. We demand that America reevaluate and rectify their extremist attitudes on the proliferation of certain nuclear holocaust. We demand that there never again be another Hiroshima or

Nagasaki." Yukio was speaking quickly and boldly. He seemed more at ease after he delivered his rendition on the salvation of mankind.

"Your people, your Friends of Humanity, have implemented unnecessary and ruthless measures of violence. If it is mankind you seek to preserve, why do you take innocent lives and threaten countless others? Why do you not seek change in the democratic way?"

"That is simple. America will not listen to peaceful means of communication or listen to intelligent reasoning. The swine in power only snub their bureaucratic noses and dig the eternal pit deeper into oblivion. Those who do not wish to listen to logic will only be satisfied when this nation and all of the world is reduced to a radioactive wasteland."

"You are mistaken, Danzai. Everything nuclear is not bad for this country or mankind. We are a peaceful nation. We seek to harm no one with our nuclear force. What we do as a nation, we do defensively. It is sad we live in a technologically advanced society that requires extreme measures for self-protection. Sad or not, it is a reality. Were it not for our nuclear strength, communism would have devoured the face of the globe. And those canisters you have inside your trailer—they are as safe as any device known to man for the transportation of hazardous nuclear waste."

Marc could tell it wasn't working. Yukio was moving nervously again and his finger was only a fraction of an inch from the detonator switch.

"You lie, pig. Our leaders are nuclear authorities. They are men of great knowledge who have studied the potential for nuclear annihilation of this planet. For your lies, you die!" The young man pushed the button on the black box and closed his eyes.

Nothing happened.

"Shit, a time delay," Marc mumbled as he came from his cover and ran toward Yukio.

There were two loud pops from inside the trailer that sounded like M-80s or giant firecrackers. Marc started to duck when he realized there would be no explosion. It was either a malfunction or Carl had gone back in and taken care of it. Marc suspected the latter.

A single shot rang from in front of Marc as he charged the man. Marc started to squeeze hard on the Uzi's trigger, but the man was already falling to the pavement. A black and bloody circle had appeared on his right temple. The left temple was gone and in its place were pieces of bloody gray matter.

Carl came from out of the darkness. "Detonators are all disengaged. The receiver is severed from the caps. I'll get this one," he shouted as he ran for the cab where Natsume Shoyo was still unconscious inside.

Marc leaned over the dead man and picked up the pistol. He locked the safety into position and tucked the weapon into his waistband.

"No problem here," Carl shouted. "This one is still breathing, but he's in bad shape. I took the Thompson."

"Let's haul ass," Marc replied. There were sirens blaring in the distance.

CHAPTER THIRTEEN

"No contact at all?" asked Ben Stacy as he pressed the talk switch on the Motorola desk microphone. "Where the hell are they?"

"Last we heard, when they were here with Agent Merrill and me, they were going to Northern California. Is it that urgent?" Captain Perry Price spoke from the control room that had been established at Edwards Air Force Base.

"I know who is involved and I suspect Gary Merrill did, too. That's why he was distracted. It cost him his life."

"Tragic," Price said.

"Okay, how long before you could have planes or choppers in the air over Northern California?"

"Three minutes. What are you thinking?"

"I'm thinking Marc and Carl aren't telling us everything they know. They went to the north part of the state for a reason. One of the bastards responsible for this has been under our noses all along."

"Who is it?" Price asked.

"I'll tell you when we meet in person. I don't trust these radios. You know scanners and electronic gadgets are cheap. Anybody could be listening," Stacy said.

"Yes, sir. Shall I deploy the aircraft?"

"Affirmative. Do it immediately. If those two guys are on to what I think they're on to, they're going to have their hands full. Some air support might come in handy if we can find them."

"Right. I'll get a couple of Cobra gunships in the sky just in case. Before I issue the order, any idea what it is we're looking for?" Price sounded almost apologetic, as if by some magic he should have known the answer before he asked the question.

"I don't know *what*, but I do know *who*. I just don't know where to find him." Stacy hesitated and then took a deep breath. "But I will find him."

Stacy cut the call off and buzzed the communications room again. Freddie answered.

"Patch me into F1. Do you know which units are active tonight?" Stacy wanted to use F1, the designated nation-wide FBI calling frequency, to contact all available FBI units. If the agents were within reasonable proximity, he wanted a mass convergence on the last known residence of the man called Mori Osamu.

"Uh, yeah. Wait a minute and I'll check the log. Hasn't been much traffic on the air tonight. Hold on, I'll have it in a second," Freddie said.

Ben Stacy held the line. He tried to be patient, but he was still quite irritated. He wondered how anything was ever accomplished on the radio with the system the way it was.

"Okay, got it," Freddie said. "There are six units in service at this time. You're ready on F1 whenever you want."

As he spoke, Stacy sat uneasily in Gary Merrill's chair and fumbled through more files. He kept the photo of Mori Osamu in front of him. His suspicion of the dissident's involvement was purely circumstantial at the moment, but he felt an interview with the man would likely change that position. And circumstantial or not, right now it was the only lead he had with any resemblance to substance.

Regardless of what an exhaustive investigation revealed. Stacy knew one thing was certain. Osamu was a living lie.

"Freddie, I want you to poll each unit individually. Once you've established contact, have the agents call me by telephone here at the office. Keep me patched in just in case I want to add something on the air. Advise each unit the telephone call is Priority One. I want those calls immediately." Stacy's voice reflected extreme urgency.

"Got it. Anything else?" Freddie asked.

"Yes. When I'm finished with the calls, meet me at the gun room. I'll need to check out several automatic weapons."

———

Mori Osamu maneuvered the stolen rig through the hairpin turns of the narrow mountain road. He reveled in the dark solitude of the high-rising mountain peaks jutting into the darkness. It was his darkness and a tool for effective completion of his one remaining purpose in life. It had long ceased to be a project where extortion money was important. It was a purpose disguised by ransom demands that truly determined the ulimate fate of all mankind. Osamu mentally surveyed the plan conceived by his own genius and that of his most trusted colleague, Nagai Soseki. He knew the government of the United States would never yield to the demands for millions of dollars. The demands had sounded legitimate when clothed in the disguise demanding an apology for involvement in the Vietnam War. He hoped the Vietnam scenario would be sufficiently distracting to cause the investigative arms of government to look in all the wrong places before any part of the puzzle fell together.

For a while, Osamu lost sight of the road in front of him. He drove by pure mechanics, his mind overwhelmed at the brilliance and insight he had brought into the project. A soothing sense of satisfaction mellowed his soul and caused him to smile. By the time the sleuths had caught scent of the proper trail, the canisters would be in place in strategic locations. It would be too late to stop the extravagant display of weakness on the part of the Nuclear Regulatory Commission and the National Transportation Safety Board.

The purpose was set. No longer would America or the world be subjected to the dark cloud of nuclear catastrophe. No longer would drivers and overroad rigs carry containers of lethal environmental poison across the highways of the country. The fuse to a new way of thinking was already lit. A new era was about to peek across the horizon of the United States and descend upon the bureaucracy. In less than twenty-four hours, all the world would know of America's constant game of Russian roulette with loaded radioactive death. The world would know. The world would see. The world would demand a change in policy, and radioactive death would no longer ride on the open back of a flatbed trailer. And what made it all so beautiful was that no one on the face of the earth could do anything at all to stop the winds of change.

Osamu rounded the final bend leading into the canyon. The encampment was well lit and people moved like ants gathering crumbs for the winter.

Osamu stopped the rig and gave the prearranged signal with his headlights. He dropped the rig back into gear and started into the encampment.

Nagai Soseki was in the area outside the cave to meet the new arrival. Osamu stopped the overroad machine and climbed from the cab.

"Greetings," Soseki said as Osamu reached the ground. "Your journey was pleasant and profitable?"

"Profitable, yes," Osamu replied. "But as for pleasant, well . . ."

"There was trouble?"

"Yes, a slight inconvenience involved with the acquisition of the rig."

"You were detected, then?"

"Yes and no. The source of my troubles is no longer among the living. Americans are a strange lot when they have their guns," Osamu said. He forced a laugh and started walking toward the mouth of the giant cave.

"Very well. You do the work of a true master." Soseki joined in stride with Osamu.

"We have the first canisters en route to their destination?" asked Osamu as the men entered the mouth of the cave.

"Yes, some time ago. They should reach their target by midmorning. We should have a call into the Environmental Protection Agency shortly before the arrival of the rig in Salt Lake City."

"Ah, yes, just in time to be too late," Osamu said. His voice was confident and his face hard.

"It will be many generations before the civilization of America forgets the stupidity of today's bureaucratic tyrants. These canisters contain the radio isotopes strontium-ninety and cesium-one-thirty-seven. It will be at least six hundred years before the isotopes decay and become stable," Soseki said.

"Yes, and it will be thousands of years before the plutonium is neutralized. The explosion of those two canisters in Salt Lake City will contain sufficient plutonium to cause extensive radiation sickness and, likely, many deaths. Perhaps then, the NRC and the deaf ears of the system will perk to attention." Osamu said as a look of satisfaction spread across his face.

"And if the radioactive contamination of one city isn't adequate to capture the necessary attention, then perhaps seeing Las Vegas as a radioactive wasteland will convince those who reside in the ivory towers," Soseki added.

"We must move the newly acquisitioned tractor-trailer into the cave and remove a sufficient amount of its cargo to make room for the canisters. I would like the rig loaded and under way on its mission before the helicopter arrives to take me back to Los Angeles," Osamu said as he looked around the cave and inspected the trolley system built by the workers for loading and unloading the canisters.

"I will see to it right away," Soseki replied. "It gives me a great deal of satisfaction to know that you and I and our fellow countrymen have taken such an active part in the transformation of American nuclear philosophy. Surely we will be remembered throughout history as merchants of mercy who ultimately saved mankind from a dismal doom. Generations throughout the world will thank us for our efficacious insight and our gallant actions."

"Yes, Nagai, you are correct. However, I fear the truckers we put out of business will not take kindly to our purpose," Osamu said laughingly.

"Let them haul animal dung," Soseki said with a stern look across his face. "It fertilizes the soil instead of sterilizing it."

Soseki and Osamu walked to a group of men who sat comfortably around a small fire inside the cave. Soseki spoke to two of the men and they immediately left the cave. It was only seconds before the idling of a diesel engine was heard outside. In less than a minute, the rig was backing into the cave for unloading.

"What is the cargo?" Soseki asked.

"I don't know. The rig wasn't marked with anything that would indicate what it was hauling. I chose it not for its cargo, but because it had just been refueled. I could find no manifests to indicate the cargo," Osamu replied.

"Interesting," Soseki said. "Shall we have a look?"

"Indeed," Osamu agreed, gesturing with his right hand for Soseki to lead the way.

Both men walked to the rear of the trailer that had stopped inside the cave. A Japanese workman was struggling with bolt cutters and attempting to cut the heavy padlock that secured the door latch. There was a loud pop and the lock fell to the dirt floor. The workman laid the bolt cutters aside and worked the latch, freeing the door. He swung the doors open and stared at the cargo. There were hundreds of boxes, each approximately twelve inches long and ten inches wide. They were about twelve inches high and stacked to the full height of the trailer. Each box was labeled; SMALL ARMS AMMUNITION.

"Incredible!" Soseki gasped. "You couldn't have done better for the purpose if you had made a methodical calculation, Mori."

"Amazing," was Osamu's only reply.

"Quickly, some of you men start unloading these cartons. Treat them gently—they contain live ammunition," Soseki said as he faced a large group of men who stared into the trailer.

"Stack them against the wall near the sleeping area," Osamu instructed. "As the boxes are unloaded, try to sort them by caliber. We may well have use of this stock before our purpose is fulfilled."

The sound of a helicopter drowned the voices inside the cave. The chopper made a pass by the huge rock crevice and then started a descent into the huge flat compound area near the barracks. It landed gently and Osamu heard the engine shut down.

"The helicopter is early or I am running late. I must be on my way. Carry on as you have thus far, Nagai. I shall await with extreme delight the outcome of your telephone call tomorrow to the EPA," Osamu said as a cold, calculating expression took possession of his face.

"It shall be done, Mori," Soseki said. "By the time the sun sets behind the horizon tomorrow, America will have experienced a lesson in learning, the magnitude of which it has never known before."

Osamu didn't speak. He bowed before Soseki, his elder, and left the cave. In seconds, the roar of the helicopter filled the cave with reverberations. The chopper lifted from the ground and disappeared into the California night.

Soseki watched the skybird until the beacon lights faded behind the mountain peaks. "Humanity will never be able to repay us, Mori Osamu," he mumbled, and then he walked back inside the cave.

———

"I understand you have a mess on your hands, Sergeant," Ben Stacy said as he spoke with the California Highway Patrol through a radio link. "But you must understand that I have one also. I have a dead agent and you have two lethal canisters of stolen nuclear waste. Those canisters are property of the United States government. I will have agents at your location in fifteen minutes. No one, but no one, is to go near those canisters. They contain highly toxic radioactive isotopes. If they're leaking, people are going to die. I don't want that, do you?"

"No, I don't want any more bodies. I already have two corpses out on Interstate Five," said Sergeant Mike Goodman.

"What? Two corpses?" Stacy interrupted the sergeant before he could finish what he was saying. "I thought you said there was a man alive in the truck."

"There is one man, an elderly Japanese, or so he appears. He is alive. We also have a woman who has been hit by a car or truck or something. Her body was in the northbound lane a couple miles from where this tractor-trailer rig crashed. Can you tell me what the hell is going on here?" Goodman asked.

"Ah, shit!" Stacy said. "Do you have any identification on the woman?"

"We're working on it. We think she may be the wife of a truck driver who was abandoned at the I-Five truckstop in Sacramento. His rig is also reported stolen. What is this, some kind of gang war or something?"

"Not exactly. As soon as you have positive I.D. on the woman, let me know. Was she Caucasian or Japanese?" asked Stacy.

"The trooper working the accident said the body was almost unrecognizable. He thinks she is Caucasian. But that isn't the worst of it."

"What are you saying?"

"The rig that disappeared an hour or so ago contained a consignment shipment of small arms ammunition. The driver reported there is probably more than a million or two rounds of live ammo in that truck," Goodman said.

"I see," Stacy said dejectedly. "What the hell is going to happen next?"

"The truck driver reported a destination of Portland, Oregon. He also said his wife was asleep in the rig's sleeper when he went into the truckstop to get some coffee. When he came out, the rig was gone and so was his wife. You know, Mr. Stacy, this sounds like some heavy stuff going down here."

"Yeah," Stacy said. "Listen, have the highway blocked off. Evacuate the area in the immediate vicinity of the crash site and keep the area clear. And one more thing—whatever it takes, keep the news media from getting around that rig and those canisters. Can you take care of that?"

"It's done," Goodman replied.

"We'll have people there shortly. Thanks for the call."

———

"This is Marc Lee. Patch me through to Agent Merrill," Marc said into the Motorola microphone.

"I wish I could, Mr. Lee, but I can't," Freddie replied over the radio link.

"What do you mean, you can't?" Marc didn't try to hide his irritation.

"Gary Merrill is dead."

"What? How?"

"A traffic accident. Burned him completely up."

"Who is in charge?"

"Ben Stacy. Hold the line and I'll patch you through to him. He was trying to reach you a little while ago."

In a few seconds, Stacy came on the air over the Department of Defense national repeater network.

"This is Stacy. Where are you?"

"I wish I could answer that," Marc said. "But I don't really know exactly. Listen, you have two canisters of waste in a wrecked truck on I-Five South just north of Sacramento. The terrorists responsible for this are part of a Japanese radical cadre."

"I know that. We have agents heading to the scene of the crash by helicopter. How did you know about it?"

"We crashed it," Marc replied. "The dead man, the young Japanese guy—he killed himself after he tried to detonate an explosive charge attached to the canisters. It didn't blow because my partner had disengaged it. These people are serious. They're going for the jugular."

"We know others we suspect of involvement. I think Gary Merrill did, too. It may have cost him his life," Stacy said sadly.

"I'm sorry to hear about that. We're going for the rest of the canisters. We'll contact you when everything is secure, and you can take it from there."

"I have air support coming into the northern part of the

state. Tell me where you are and I'll have backup to you in minutes," Stacy said.

"Sorry . . . we're losing the repeater. You're breaking up. We'll contact you when we have the canisters. Lee out."

"Mr. Lee, do you read me? You can't do this alone. It's suicide. Do you read me?" Stacy's voice crackled over the radio speaker.

Marc reached to the control head of the transceiver and turned the volume control down.

"That's one way to keep interference down." Carl drove the rig through the night and soon the sign appeared beside the highway that indicated the exit they sought. Carl turned the rig onto the exit and left the interstate super-highway.

"I think we should do it like we discussed earlier, Marc said.

"We have plenty of rope and maybe a dozen or two rockets for the Light Antitank Weapon. It looked like a lot of trigger fingers in that place. Stacy might be right. It could be suicide."

"We've taken on worse odds. My biggest concern is the canisters. If they get opened or ruptured, it's over."

"Yeah, for all of us."

Fifteen minutes passed and the rig threaded its way along the narrow gravel road leading into the encampment. When the Delta Warriors were near the top of the last ridge leading to the canyon floor, Carl stopped. The road rose steadily ahead of them and made a hairpin curve to the right as it started its descent into the encampment. It was a mile to the mouth of the cave and the roadway fell through a steep grade along the walls of high mountain peaks. It was the only road access into or out of the canyon. The road on each side was surrounded by treacherous rock pinnacles, some with drop-offs over a hundred feet. Anyone leaving the encampment by road would have to drive over Marc and Carl's overroad rig—or through it.

Marc jumped from the cab and went to the back of the trailer. He opened the doors and slid the ramps into place. Carl quickly joined him and started the Jeep Cherokee. He cautiously backed the Jeep down the ramps and onto the dirt road surface.

Marc placed the ramps back inside the trailer and closed the doors. Carl left the Jeep idling and went back to the cab of the rig. He dropped the gearshift into low and moved the rig crossways on the dirt road, effectively blocking any escape from the killing ground on the other side of the mountain peaks.

"Let's do a fast weapons check and go kick some ass," Marc said as Carl joined him at the rear of the Cherokee.

"Let's get it done," Carl replied as he pulled back the charging lever on his Uzi and let it slam closed.

CHAPTER FOURTEEN

Marc and Carl threaded their way through the steep terrain. The Cherokee had been effectively hidden in the dense undergrowth beside the access road. It was insurance for their escape in the event the rig was trashed in an escape attempt by some bold souls from the encampment.

The night was still, the silence broken only by the occasional call of some roving night birds and the sound of Marc and Carl's footsteps as they weaved their way toward the encampment.

A sudden and unexpected burst of sound sent the night warriors to the ground for cover. A helicopter appeared over the towering mountain peaks and flew immediately from sight toward the southwest.

"Where the hell did that come from?" Carl asked.

"Either bringing supplies into the encampment or taking something out," Marc whispered.

"Great. Let's hope they were bringing something in. I sure would like to wrap this mess up before morning," Carl said.

"Yeah." Marc got up and continued walking toward the rock cliffs surrounding the encampment.

"Think our sentry will be back?" Carl said.

"He's out here somewhere. All we have to do is find him before he finds us. As sloppy as he was earlier, he isn't much threat unless we spook him and he opens fire. If we have to fire shots before we're ready, we'll have a whole army of these crazies down on us."

"How's the shoulder?" Carl asked.

"It hurts, but I can still use it. It won't slow me down," Marc replied.

The men continued through the night. The sky was filled with crisp air and dotted with tiny white stars. There was no moon and the mountainous terrain caused the darkness to be nothing but blackness. The warriors moved slowly and cautiously, stopping every few feet to listen for the sounds of anyone else on the high ridges. So far, they had heard nothing since the helicopter vanished into the black night.

Each man carried a Mini maglite but neither dared use it. It would be nothing more than a beacon for even a poor marksman. And if the shooter had an automatic weapon, it would be difficult to miss the source of the light.

Marc paused for a brief rest, his breathing already becoming heavy from the load of the equipment pack and the thin, cool air. He sat on a large boulder, dropped the Uzi from its sling on his shoulder, and laid it across his lap. "Brother, if I don't come out of this hellhole, you and Brittin be sure to take care of Jill for me. Will you do that?"

"Shit! That doesn't sound like the eternal optimist. Anyway, what makes you think I'll come out if you don't?"

Marc didn't answer.

"We'll both come— " Carl didn't finish. The sound of a twig snapping in the night cut him short. He crouched down, hugging the ground.

Marc was beside him, and the Uzi snapped forward in his hands. Neither warrior spoke.

The sound continued. Another twig snapped and then came the sound of a rock tumbling down a perch and slamming into a larger rock. The sound reverberated into the night with a resonate thud and clacking echo.

The Delta Warriors could see the man now. He was ahead of them and to their right nearly seventy-five yards. He stood out like a homing beacon on a lighthouse, a burning cigarette dangling from his hand in the darkness. The red-orange tip glowed, and then the beacon became brighter as the man placed it between his lips and inhaled.

The sentry was moving, coming directly at Marc and Carl. The warriors slipped closer to the ground. The sentry had obviously missed the sounds of the warriors moving and their voices whispering in the darkness. He moved without caution, content either in his abilities or the safety of his assignment.

Marc reached to his left hip and gently unsnapped the giant Parker-Imai survival knife. He quietly laid the Uzi on the ground and gripped the cold metal handle of the awesome knife with his right hand. The sentry kept coming. His cigarette had returned to a dull glow and Marc could smell the smoke now as it floated on the air toward him.

Marc and Carl waited, and with the roll of a rock beneath the approaching man's feet Carl slipped the safety off on his Uzi. His sound-suppressed automatic weapon was trained on the shape moving through the night. At the face of the closed bolt on the handy little subgun, a 115-grain hollow-point projectile waited for launch to strike the life from the sentry.

The man was closing the gap now, his stride slow and casual. He wasn't more than twenty yards away. The cigarette was burning down and the man took a final draw from it. He flicked the burning beacon to the ground and stepped on it. The smoke exhaled by the man sailed into the darkness and drifted across Marc and Carl. The man coughed and then cleared his throat. He spat hard onto the ground and started walking again.

The warriors waited. The man was ten yards away . . .

five . . . Marc sprang to his feet, the gleaming Parker-Imai poised in his right fist. The man frantically struggled for his weapon, but he was too late. Nine and a half inches of cold and lethal steel found flesh beneath the guard's ribcage. Marc plunged the razor-sharp blade into his victim's chest cavity.

The sentry tried to scream but Marc's left hand found his mouth and covered it. There was a gurgling sound as Marc twisted the cold steel and slashed all life from the man. His body stiffened, quivered, and then crumpled toward the ground. Marc jerked the knife free of the dead man's chest and raked it across his throat for good measure as the body collapsed to the rocks.

Marc pulled the knife back, ready to strike again; but the man was already on his journey to eternity. Marc loosened his grip on the knife handle and wiped the blade clean on the dead man's jacket. He slipped the deadly fighting knife back into its sheath and picked up the dead man's automatic assault rifle.

Carl was beside him now. "You're bad with that blade, dude. I'm glad you're on my side," he whispered.

"Yeah, it's not always that easy; you know that."

"And thanks to this guy, we're committed now. What say we go finish what we've started?"

Marc didn't say anything. He started walking on toward the crest of the cliffs surrounding the encampment. The rocky terrain would have challenged a mountain goat, but the Delta Warriors made their way with caution and cunning.

They reached the edge of the rocks overlooking the encampment floor. The area was unchanged from their visit hours earlier, with the exception of a new eighteen-wheel rig protruding from the cave mouth. The area around the cave and barracks looked like a giant bowl. It was surrounded by high jutting cliffs with only one exit: the narrow road that led back to the main highway. From the ambient light below, Marc could see a giant outcrop of rock hanging over the road twenty or thirty yards from the level camp floor. The mouth of the cave was at his right, a hundred and fifty yards from the road.

"My guess is there will be a guard on that outcropping to the left," Marc said. "I think we need to move around the upper perimeter and thin the guards. We can set some charges and cause a little more instant havoc."

"Sounds good. Maybe we should split up and move in from two different directions."

"When we go in, the first thing we have to eliminate is the communications shack over by the barracks. We need to eliminate any possibility for contact with the outside world. A rocket should do it."

"If the charges are set and detonated just right, we can take the place and shut this operation down in a matter of minutes," Carl added.

"Let's move on the guards together, and then we can split up as we go in."

"Say when, Colonel."

"Let's do it."

Both men were on their feet and moving swiftly, yet cautiously, across the canyon rim. They etched their way around the rocky peaks, searching for the lookouts they knew would be lurking somewhere in the darkness. In less than ten minutes, their hunch paid off. A guard, casually sitting on a huge boulder with his assault rifle on his lap, didn't detect the movement of the Delta Warriors.

Marc covered with his silenced Uzi. Carl moved on the man. The guard watched the few men moving in the encampment below. Carl slipped behind the man, moving across the face of the rock with the cunning of a giant cat. In one massive lunge, Carl covered the distance between the edge of the rock and the guard.

The man turned just as Carl threw a front snap kick into his face.

Carl's foot caught the man under the chin and lifted him from the rock. His assault rifle disappeared into the darkness. The terrorist guard was stunned and injured before he knew what hit him. But the man came up spitting and gasping for air. Carl moved on him again. This time a lunge-punch combination caught the man in the face and the chest at the same time. The man fell back and reached for a knife. Carl came forward with his own Parker-Imai slashing air before the guard could find his balance. Then the gleaming surgical steel blade ripped through flesh on the man's chest. The guard tried to scream, but Carl was already feeling steel penetrate flesh on the backswing as the huge survival knife severed the guard's throat. The body slumped to the rock, the man's final scream drowned by his own blood.

Carl stepped over the fallen guard and wiped his blade clean on the man's pants. He kicked the knife from the dead man's fingers, grabbed his shirt collar, and dragged the body from the rock. Marc was beside him now and helped conceal the body beneath the giant rock.

Marc rummaged through his backpack and found two explosive charges and digital radio receivers. He secured the timers to the face of the rock overhang towering above the canyon floor. He punched up a frequency selection on the receiver-detonators and energized the units.

It had been less than two minutes since the fracas started with the guard. The warriors were under way again.

The search for more guards lasted another thirty minutes. Two more guards were found and each was easily dispatched.

Marc placed a total of twelve charges in strategic locations around the canyon rim. It took fifteen more minutes to reach the outcropping that Marc and Carl had

ed as their first observation point. The men quickly
cured ropes to trees near the canyon rim and dropped the
pe bundles over the edge.

"Break out the LAW and let's liven up the night," Marc
id once the rope chore was completed.

Carl took the LAW in his hands, charged it with a 66mm
cket, and lifted the awesome little weapon to his shoul-
r. "The guard and the overhang over the road first?" Carl
ghted the two-foot tube at the rock ledge.

"Once we start, we'll have to move fast. Put the second
e into the communications shack and then we'll go in."
arc moved to Carl's left to avoid contact with the lethal
caping gases from the rocket launcher that would flash
veral feet behind Carl when he fired.

"Right. Just say when, boss."

"Let's start the show," Marc said evenly.

Carl fingered the firing mechanism on the LAW. A loud
hoosh broke the silence and a glowing trail of fire spiraled
ward the rock outcropping at lightning speed. The 66mm
ght antitank rocket slammed into the rock with an explo-
ve and fiery flash. An earth-shattering roar brought the
nyon to life. The huge rock fragmented into dump
uck–sized boulders and plummeted into the roadbed
low. The shattering sounds of crumbling, shattered rock
hoed throughout the canyon long after the sound of the
plosion drifted away. The falling rock blocked the road-
ay with such effectiveness that it would take a skilled
nstruction crew with heavy equipment several weeks to
ake it passable again.

Marc moved to reload the rocket launcher. Carl spun
ound quickly and placed the second explosive projectile
to the communications shack before the rocks stopped
lling from the first impact. The glowing trail marked the
ay to destruction as the projectile slapped into the
ooden frame building. In a microsecond, the communi-

cations shack and Izumi Shimada disappeared from the fac
of the earth in the middle of a raging, fiery burst.

The compound was alive now. Men ran from the cave
Some of them were armed and fumbling with their weapon
as they searched for a target. Others simply looked stunne
as they gawked at the massive destruction inflicted on the
hideout in a matter of seconds.

Marc and Carl were on the ropes and rappelling dow
the face of the cliffs before the fire died from the commu
nications shack. They found the ground on the surface
the compound.

Marc moved first as he unsnapped the D-ring that ha
secured him to the ropes. He ran for cover, ducking in an
out of rock shelters. There was no gunfire yet. The men i
the compound were stunned and they still hadn't found
target.

Carl was moving around the compound to Marc's le
when gunfire started. Bullets ricocheted off the rocks ove
Carl's head. He went down on his stomach and sprea
eagled on the ground. Automatic weapons fire was heav
now as a small army of men fired at the same time. Th
bullets pelted into the rocks and evaporated into dust.

Carl came up when the gunfire paused. He unleashed
burst from the Uzi. The silent sizzlers found several bodie
of receptive flesh among the men who had been firin
toward him. He saw at least three men crumble to th
ground, killed by silent and deadly 9mm hollow points.

The radicals were undeterred. They moved toward th
face of the rocky peaks in a wave. Carl raised up again an
fired out the Uzi. Two more men fell into screaming deatl
but the shooters kept coming.

Marc was up, lending support fire from a hidde
position behind more large rocks. His 9mm Uzi subgu
belched hot death into the human wave. Bodies fell an
men screamed, but the terrorists didn't slow down. Th

Delta Warrior's silent sizzlers were answered with heavy assault rifle fire as rock chips and lead fragments rained down on them like a hailstorm.

Carl found a fragmentation grenade, squeezed the spoon against the body, and yanked the pin free. He dropped back into long-arm form and tossed the frag pineapple into the wave of men. The explosion ripped through the assaulters, sending weapons, clothing, and burning human flesh sailing in a rain of doom.

The survivors kept coming toward the rock wall and Carl.

Marc dumped his Uzi, buttoned down the empty stick, and slammed a fresh one up the well. He slapped back the charging lever and stripped a round into the chamber. He stood this time, firing the Uzi in highly controlled three-round bursts.

The fanatics returned fire toward him now. Even as Japanese bodies fell, the main thrust of the human wave was undaunted.

Marc fired out the new stick and let the Uzi drop to his side on the sling. He came around with an M-16, thumbed the safety off, and spat .223-caliber death into the crowd of crazed terrorists. He dumped a thirty-round magazine in quick three-round bursts. Bodies fell from his wave of hot flying death pellets.

Carl was firing again with his left hand gripped around the pistol grip of the Uzi while his right hand fumbled through his musette bag for another hand grenade. He found one, pulled the pin with his teeth, and threw the handheld explosive into the assailants.

More bodies and ripped flesh sailed into the sky with a cloud of dirt and rock. But now there was a new sound drowning out the sound of gunfire. It was a helicopter swooping low over the canyon rim. The chatter of assault rifle fire dwindled and faded as hard-hitting machine gun fire flashed from the chopper. The bullets dug furrows into the California ground inside the compound as the chopper made a strafing run, banked hard left, and cleared the treacherous mountain peaks.

"Where the hell did that come from?" Carl mumbled aloud as the chopper returned and unleashed a ferocious two-second burst of machine gun fire into the advancing terrorists.

The chopper climbed and then banked again. The pilot brought the bird in for another run, and when he disappeared there were no Japanese gunmen left standing. The Cobra gunship dispatched by Captain Price vanished as quickly as it had come.

Marc and Carl cleared cover at the same time. Both men ran for the mouth of the cave. There was no warning when the roar of the overroad rig's diesel engine filled the mouth of the cave and bounced from the walls of the canyon. The rig leapt forward awkwardly as the trailer cleared the cave. Marc and Carl emptied the sticks from their M-16s into the cab of the rig. The diesel bucked and jerked and finally stopped a hundred feet from the cave.

There was a new menace—several dozen armed men standing in the mouth of the cave. One man stood alone in front of the others by several feet. He was armed only with a Thompson submachine gun.

"Stop where you are—whoever you are. If you come closer, we will detonate the nuclear waste canisters. There are ten canisters inside this cave, more than enough to destroy the environment of Northern California for thousands of years!" the man shouted. It was Nagai Soseki.

"You have no escape," Marc yelled. "That was a military Cobra gunship that wiped out your first line of defense. If he comes back, there will be no survivors. Surrender and you will not be harmed. Enough people have died already."

"Yes, what you say is true. Enough people have died.

pparently there hasn't been enough death for America to hange its way of thinking," Soseki yelled.

"What are you saying? Why are you doing this?" asked Marc.

"Your trucks, your eighteen-wheelers as you call them. ou permit the transportation of nuclear death across the ighways of this country with little or no protection and ven less restriction for travel in populated areas. You take his death and bury it. In doing so, you rape the environnent even more. You Americans haven't seen, as we apanese have, the excruciating results of nuclear energy inleashed. Nuclear proliferation must cease."

"This isn't the way to accomplish your desire for change. Killing innocent people as you have done is not the way to insure change. That isn't the way of democracy."

"Your way for change is in error. America will not be eceptive to change of their ways until the world is lestroyed. Is that the way of your democracy?"

"You are mistaken, Mister. What is your name?"

"I am Nagai Soseki. I am a professor of nuclear studies. am a respected expert in the field of nuclear energy. I am iot mistaken. I know what I say is true."

"Mr. Soseki," Carl said. "Please, there is no reason for inyone else to die here tonight. Enough blood has been hed. Your point has been proven."

"Liar!" Soseki shouted. "Even if you kill all of us, there s another truck with two canisters headed for another najor American city. It will detonate automatically upon irrival at its destination."

"No, Soseki. We stopped that rig on Interstate Five a couple hours ago. The old man is unconscious and the oung driver is dead. By now the canisters are back in the iands of government officials. Please surrender," Marc pleaded.

Soseki hesitated, and then he spoke. "There is well over

one million rounds of ammunition in this cave. I will detonate it and the canisters, if need be. I will bring this mountain down on all of us and send the isotopes of death into the atmosphere before I will surrender. Mankind is too important."

"Back up very slowly," Marc whispered to Carl. "When I say *now*, fire a rocket into those cartons inside the cave. I'm going to start some fireworks."

Marc and Carl started moving back from the confrontation. "Mr. Soseki, my partner and I are backing off. You have free passage from the canyon. You win!" Marc shouted.

"Another American trick. I may just blow the canisters anyway," Soseki retorted.

Marc and Carl were a hundred yards from the mouth of the cave. "Now!" Marc said.

Carl dropped to one knee, sighted instantly, and launched the rocket toward the cartons of ammunition inside the cave.

Marc slapped at the transmitter switches on the radio-controlled detonators.

It was impossible to determine which explosion came first. The mountain erupted like a volcano. Fire and debris filled the night sky and rained down on the canyon floor. At the same instant, the rocket hit the ammunition inside the cave. Fire belched from the cave mouth as the men standing in its way turned instantly into cinders. Before the flames could completely lick from the cave, millions of tons of hard rock crashed to the canyon floor in an avalanche that seemed to never end.

Eternity came in a matter of seconds. The stolen canisters of deadly nuclear waste and the remains of the Friends of Humanity were forever sealed harmlessly inside the bowels of the hard rock mountain.

CHAPTER FIFTEEN

It was nearly ten o'clock in the morning when Marc, Carl, and Ben Stacy walked into the office of the Environmental Protection Agency in Los Angeles.

"Good morning, Mr. Yasunari," Stacy said. "This is Mr. Lee and Mr. Browne. They are special investigators for the NRC. I thought you might like to meet them."

Jim Yasunari stood behind his desk and extended a hand to Marc and then Carl. He smiled as Carl shook his hand. When the smile filled Yasunari's face, Carl thought what a nice gold incisor Jim Yasunari had.

"I trust you fine gentlemen are here in anticipation of another telephone contact from the people who are threatening to terrorize this country," Yasunari said.

"Actually, we're here to remove the telephone bugging equipment," Stacy replied.

"Oh? Has the material been recovered?"

"Covered, yes. Recovered, no," Marc said evenly.

"I don't believe I understand," Yasunari said.

"I'm sure you don't," Stacy said. "But maybe Mori Osamu does understand. Would that be an accurate evaluation?"

Yasunari was unmoved. "What are you saying? You aren't making any sense. Who is Mori Osamu?"

"Nice try," Stacy said as his Model 13 Smith & Wesson cleared leather. "Mori Osamu, alias Jim Yasunari, I have a federal warrant for your arrest. Your game is over. Most of your comrades in the Friends of Humanity are dead. You're all alone."

"It was you leaving in the helicopter last night," Marc said with ice in his eyes. "Your fingerprints are all over the stolen tractor-trailer we found at the abandoned encampment. They match the prints we took in this office—your prints.

"I will also have California state warrants charging you with murder, kidnapping, and grand theft auto in the death of Janie Jackson," Stacy said. "You've done well with your double life, but it's all over now. Put your hands on top of your head and step this way."

Marc put his hand into the small of his back and wrapped his fingers around the grip of the double-action Beretta 92F 9mm auto. He stood poised and ready to deal with the terrorist killer in front of him.

Osamu hesitated and then did as he had been instructed. He placed his hands on top of his head and walked from behind his desk.

"Lie down on the floor and extend your arms in front of you," Stacy instructed.

Osamu complied.

Stacy moved beside Osamu and grabbed one of his wrists. He placed a handcuff on it and then cuffed the other wrist. He searched the radical terrorist and then assisted him to his feet. Then he read the Miranda rights and looked Osamu squarely in the face. "I just have one question Osamu. Why?"

"The transportation of nuclear materials to unsafe disposition sites in this country must cease. American is flirting with eternal damnation of the entire globe by unrestricted and unsafe contamination of the environment with nuclear proliferation. The purpose will be served . . . mankind will be saved. The loss of a few lives is insignificant in the salvation of all humanity. Where I have left off, others will someday follow. America must make the transition from nuclear doom to a safe way of life for all mankind. The lives that have departed our presence are unimportant in the overall scope of things," Osamu said confidently.

"Tell that to Gary Merrill's wife and children, or maybe Artlie Anders's widow," Stacy said, and he escorted Osamu from the room as Marc and Carl watched.

They were through the door to Osamu's office when the man's feet moved with the speed of a lightning bolt. He was on his toes, his left foot pivoting right a full 360 degrees and his right foot airborne. The crest of the flying foot struck Stacy in the side of his head at the temple. The FBI agent slammed into the wall and fell to the floor. Osamu completed another spin and grabbed the doorknob to his office with his handcuffed hands. He slammed it closed.

Marc and Carl moved at the same time. They ran for the door and opened it with a jerk. Osamu's feet flashed through the doorway with a right-left combination front snap kick.

The Delta Warriors ducked and the kicks missed. The door slapped shut again and Marc drew the Beretta. He thumbed down the safety and stood back from the door as Carl drew it open.

There was nothing there except Stacy, unconscious on the floor.

The Delta Warriors were in the hall with a half-roll and then on their feet. Osamu had disappeared.

A scream came from the outer office at the end of the hallway. The sound had hardly reached Marc and Carl's ears before they were running toward it. They made the turn into the office, but Osamu was already gone. A petite young black secretary stood beside the door screaming.

Osamu was into the main hallway leading to the outside.

He was running smoothly, his arms still cuffed behind his back. He stopped briefly, inhaled deeply, and thrust the focus of all of his body's energy into his wrists.

He willed his mind to cause the handcuffs to snap. He flexed his shoulders and sent the mental energy to the ends of his arms. In a mighty burst, the links binding the two handcuffs ruptured. He reached into the lining of his belt and found a thin spring steel lock pick hidden there. He slipped the device from its sheath and inserted it into the handcuff on his left wrist. He slid the thin device between the lock lip and the serrated jaw of the cuff. He flicked his wrist and the cuff jaw sprang free. He quickly repeated the procedure on his other wrist, freeing it also. Osamu dropped the broken cuffs to the floor and laughed out loud. His hands were free and he started running again.

Osamu cleared the outer door to the street as Marc and Carl burst through the last office door. They ran hard and gained ground on the fleeing felon.

Osamu was into the open on the sidewalk. He spotted a beat patrolman walking away from him. He ran for the lawman, reaching him in four giant strides. The unsuspecting officer turned slightly just as Osamu came down on him with an open-handed blow to the base of his cranium. The officer fell to the sidewalk dead, his neck broken.

Osamu grabbed the dead lawman's revolver and pulled it free of leather. He unsnapped one of two speed loader pouches and grabbed the HKS speed loader. He stuffed it into his pocket and started running again.

Marc and Carl spotted the fallen patrolman as they burst through the doors into the street. Marc dropped to a crouch and yelled for Osamu to stop. The fleeing man pivoted on one foot and fired a wild shot at Marc. Marc aimed the auto pistol to return fire. He squeezed gently on the trigger of the Beretta, but he held it. A pedestrian was across the street behind Osamu. A missed shot could have killed the innocent bystander.

Osamu vanished from sight, but reappeared an instant later. He was clinging to the back of a slow-moving tractor-trailer rig and coming straight at Marc and Carl.

Carl snapped off a double-tap from his Beretta. Osamu jerked back around the rear of the trailer. The shots missed and tore metal as they crashed into the frame of the trailer where Osamu's head had been an instant before.

The driver of the rig was oblivious to Osamu's presence until the shots were fired by Carl. When he saw the two men on the sidewalk aiming weapons toward his rig, he slammed on the air brakes and screeched the huge eighteen-wheeler to a stop.

Osamu was off the trailer before it stopped. He hit the pavement and weaved his way through the traffic. Tires screeched and horns blared as he caused the vehicular flow to all but stop. A large sanitation vehicle approached in the oncoming lane, going the opposite way the tractor-trailer had been going. Osamu jumped for the vehicle and grabbed a railing at the back. He climbed on top of the huge truck and sat straddling a single railing that ran the width of the truck at the back end. He spotted Marc and Carl running along the sidewalk.

Osamu aimed and then fired just as the truck shifted gears. His shot went wild and struck a window in a building behind Marc and Carl.

Carl was down in a semicrouch. The Beretta was in his hands and pointed toward Osamu. He worked the trigger and the Beretta belched out a pair of double-taps. Carl saw Osamu fall backward, his body lurching from the impact of the 9mm hellfire. He vanished into the open top of the sanitation truck just as the driver-operator worked the hydraulic compactor to compress his assorted load of garbage into a firm solid mass of refuse.

The sanitation truck continued moving to the next intersection a hundred yards away. The driver turned the truck right onto another street. The huge sanitation vehicle disappeared from view and continued on its way to dump the load at a thermal electrical generation incinerator.

———

The flight back to Washington, D.C., had been pleasant enough. The white Learjet had covered the continent in a relatively short time. The time in flight had given Marc and Carl an opportunity to assess the effectiveness of the mission. Stacy had regained consciousness and was extremely irritated that he had missed the chance to terminate Osamu. There had been no identification numbers on the back of the sanitation vehicle, and once it had been located through a complicated process of elimination, the vehicle had already dumped its refuse into the thermal incinerator. Mori Osamu was gone, but his actions and those of the Friends of Humanity would linger for generations.

The Friends of Humanity had proven to be an isolated radical group operating without any known connection with the Japanese government or Japanese people. They had dedicated themselves to a cause of change through violence. The participants in the radical terror group had, through their heritage, experienced the effects of nuclear devastation. Their deranged efforts led not only to their downfall, but to their extinction as well.

In the two weeks that had passed since the Delta Warriors left the killing fields of California, Congress had enacted legislation to change the regulations concerning the disposition of nuclear waste. Trucking companies that secured government hauling contracts were required to enact stringent security measures before moving nuclear waste across America's highways. And although the method had been nothing short of madness, the purpose of the terrorist transgressions had caused new inroads to be carved in the way America handled nuclear materials. And for that, perhaps all of the deaths in California had not been in vain.

The National Transportation Safety Board had ordered a new series of intensive tests on the canisters used to haul nuclear waste. The results proved that the titanium canisters currently in use were virtually indestructible and thus quite adequate for the transportation of the materials.

A team of nuclear disposal specialists and geologists examined the cave in Northern California where the remaining ten canisters had been entombed. The team unanimously pronounced the tomb forever sealed and the canisters harmlessly disposed of.

Marc had used his time wisely since his return to Washington. He had spent most of it with Jill after a short one-day flight to Dallas to see his father, who still found peace in the sleep. Jill had left for Georgia and the training that would cause her to view life differently when she returned.

Carl and Marc had put in exhausting hours in the design of the new overroad rig that would be their base of operations throughout the United States in their new found sanctioned war on crime. The engineers and designers had been extremely cooperative and exhaustive in each detail for the one-of-a-kind rig. And the president had kept his promise . . . he had spared no expense in the construction of the war machine.

Marc and Carl were with the chief design engineer in a dismal warehouse in the southern section of Alexandria, Virginia. The rig was completed and it was time for the final rundown on weapons, operating systems, and capabilities. It was a day Marc and Carl had longed for since they agreed to accept the president's offer. And at last that day had come.

"Gentlemen, if you're ready, we'll give this fighting machine the once-over," T. K. Davidoff said. He was a mild-mannered man in his mid-forties. His hair was balding on top and he wore thick wire-rimmed glasses. The chief engineer was inherently assertive and he always spoke fast. Davidoff held to the invalid assumption that those he spoke with had brains that moved as quickly as his. He also felt as much pride as Marc and Carl in the completion of the overroad rig. It had been his most extensive and expedient project since he had locked hands with the federal government. It had also been his greatest challenge since he received his doctorate in engineering.

"Let's run her through once," Marc said. He had a boyish smile across his normally hard face. There was a slight gleam in his eyes as he realized that the machine he and Carl had dreamed of had become reality.

"I'm ready." Carl was as excited as a child anticipating a new toy.

Davidoff opened a walkway door into the dark warehouse. He stopped to switch on a circuit breaker. The giant room flooded with clear white light that resembled sunshine.

The rig sat in the center of the huge room. It shone and glittered on every turn of its slick outer skin. The cab was a huge Class 8 painted fire-engine red. A double sleeper extended from the back of the cockpit and rose into a natural drag spoiler with twin windows towering above the cab. A pair of gleaming chrome stacks rose from the back of the sleeper, one on each side of the cab. The nose of the cab was of aerodynamic design and it appeared that some machine had thrown the best of current designs into a pot and produced the end result. There was no manufacturer's logo above the solid chrome radiator. Instead, a shiny oval engraved nameplate read, OVERLOAD.

The new rig looked like any typical modern overroad rig from all outward appearances, but appearance is where any similarities ended. Inside, the rig was a custom-designed, long-range fighting machine.

"Wow!" Carl said excitedly. "I can't wait to get this baby on the road."

"It's beautiful," Marc agreed.

"Here is a compilation of the final design specifications." Davidoff handed a copy of the manual to Marc and Carl. "If you'll thumb through those specs with me, I'll run this machine down for you."

Marc opened the first page. It was stamped in red ink: TOP SECRET. He thumbed on to the first specification page.

"Okay," Davidoff said evenly. "This is a custom tractor with a very special 1,400-horsepower diesel engine. The engine was especially designed for this project by a government-contracted subsidiary of Caterpillar. The engine is fed from a pair of traditional fuel tanks on each side of the cab. There is also a fuel link to the undercarriage of the trailer which is designed with aircraft-type tanks capable of carrying an extra thousand gallons of fuel.

"That translates into a nonstop trip from New York to California and back again without a fuel stop. The tanks are lined on the bottom side with a high-tensile and ultradensity metallic substance lighter than aluminum. The remarkable density of this metal will resist anything but a direct hit from an air-to-surface missile. The outer skin of the trailer is also made from this top-secret material. The versatility of this thin metal is phenomenal. We call the stuff Armorshield; it's a lot easier than the scientific name."

"Wow!" Carl said again. "Keep going."

"The interior of the cab looks just like a normal rig. You do have, however, a complete computer and communications link to the trailer by way of high-tech fiber optics. The entire run of the complex operating systems is no larger than the diameter of a small common nail. Backup communications systems are installed beneath the twin seats, and the seats sit on air shock absorbers. You can operate the rig with the trailer or run bobtail and still have more than ample communications facilities."

"What's in the communications network?" Marc asked.

"You name it, it's in there. Most of the communications system is housed in the front end of the trailer. Without boring you with the minute specifics, suffice it to say that you have the capability of covering any frequency from below standard broadcast to well inside the K-band microwave links. You also have internal and portable VHF and UHF repeaters for fixed and mobile operation. As you can see, no antennas are visible besides the pair of inconspicuous CB antennas on the cab.

"Your UHF, VHF, and K-band links feed flat-plate antennas mounted in the roof of both the cab and the trailer. None but the closest inspection would ever reveal them. It's exactly the same kind of system you might find on the White House communications van."

"Remarkable," Marc said in awe.

"Trust me," Davidoff said. "You'll like it even more when you get these goodies out on the road and start utilizing some of their applications."

"I trust you," Carl said.

"Let's go to the trailer. You're going to like this, I'm sure." Davidoff walked to the rear of the rig and opened the double doors.

"Damn, man, look at those Jeeps," Carl said as he eyed the two new Jeep Cherokees inside the trailer. One was red and the other black.

"Look closely," Davidoff added. "You've never seen anything quite like them. They aren't your average Cher-

okees, except on the outside. The four-liter engines have
been removed and replaced with three-fifty-cubic-inch
LT-One Corvette engines of seventies vintage. That, of
course, was your request, Colonel Lee. The engines are
new and we tested these machines on the salt flats in Utah
the day before yesterday. The digital speedometer locked
out at two hundred miles per hour. In short, these mothers
would fly if they had wings. The outer bodies are also of
Armorshield. All glass in both the tractor and the Cherokees is a Corning bullet-resistant variety just like we use on
the presidential limo. You have three antennas showing
here. One, the cowl mount up front, is for the AM/FM
radio in the dashboard, and the other two roof mounts are
Maxrad UHF and VHF five-eighths wave base-loaded
stainless steel whips that are broad-banded across a wide
spectrum of frequencies. As you can see, the loading ramps
for the vehicles are hydraulic and they completely disappear into the floor of the trailer when they aren't needed."

"Sounds wonderful," Marc said. "What about weapons?"

"Let's go inside the trailer first. I have a couple of
special surprises for you in there. When we finish with that,
I'll cover the tactical weapons systems."

Davidoff pressed a concealed switch inside the doors
and the ramp extended to full length and settled to the
concrete floor. All three men walked into the trailer and
passed the custom Jeep Cherokees. A long wall ran the
length of the trailer and extended to the ceiling at a
forty-five-degree angle. A pair of Honda four-by-four all-
terrain vehicles sat on the slanted wall.

"All right!" Carl said eagerly when he saw the ATVs.

"More than all right," Davidoff said. "These vehicles are
equipped with steerable twin rocket pods. They will fire
sixty-six-millimeter light antitank rockets of the LAW family. There is also a pair of belt-fed seven-point-six-two light

machine guns. The belts and ammo containers are beneath the undercarriage of the vehicle. The power plants for the machines have been extensively modified. These little beauties have a ground speed capability of over one hundred miles per hour."

"Wonderful." Marc shook his head in amazement.

"Yeah, but don't get yourselves killed on them. They'll still roll over quite easily. I suggest you play with them awhile before you try any heroics."

"You have our word," Carl said.

"Now, I'll continue," Davidoff said. "Beyond this wall is the communications and comfort zone. You have a full and massive array of communications equipment. We'll go into more detail when you've had a chance to play with it. You also have long-term living quarters. It may be a little cramped, but it's damned efficient. Water and gasoline tanks are mounted in the ceiling for gravity flow. Sewerage tanks are below the undercarriage at the end of the diesel fuel ballasts. There are two silenced and concealed generators that will run the systems when you are in a fixed location, or one of them may be used while you're on the road. You'll find more goodies when you review the manual in-depth. Now, Colonel Lee, you asked about weapons systems?"

"That's right," Marc said.

"I'll review them briefly. You have six front-mounted light machine guns. There is also a pair of twenty millimeter cannons on the front. There are four forward and six rear rocket pods that retract and conceal. There are four machine guns on the rear, and they are steerable to each side of the rig. They are aimed through infrared and fiber-optic technology. Essentially, all weapons may be operated from the cab or the control center in the trailer by closed-circuit television and infrared fiber optics. You can fight a small war without ever leaving your bunks if you want to."

"You think we're smart enough to learn how to operate all this stuff?" asked Carl.

"We'll work it out," replied Marc with a sheepish grin.

"Rather than discuss the details any further, I think you'd be better served to experience the magic of this machine in full operation. We can pick up the review and questions another day. Is that agreeable?" Davidoff asked as a telephone bell echoed through the warehouse.

"Sounds great," Marc said. "Why don't you catch your telephone?"

Davidoff walked to a telephone extension on the wall at the side of the warehouse and answered it.

"It's for you guys. There's another extension in the office. The president would like to speak to both of you."

Marc and Carl answered simultaneously.

"Good morning, gentlemen," the president said. "I hope you are pleased with what you see. It fulfills your basic request—with a little polish. I trust this sixteen-million-dollar piece of equipment will make your transition from Delta Force Warriors to Highway Warriors a little bit easier."

"No doubt about it." Marc said.

"I second that, Mr. President," Carl said.

"Good. Use it wisely and make this country safe again. We're all counting on you."

ABOUT THE AUTHOR

Bob Ham was raised in the Blue Ridge Mountains, just outside Roanoke, Virginia. He attended college in Roanoke and later studied law.

Bob has an extensive background in law enforcement, with experience ranging from traffic patrol to highly detailed undercover operations involving narcotics and firearms.

In the mid-seventies, he relocated to Nashville, Tennessee, where he gave up law enforcement for a successful career in the country music business. Bob now owns a record promotion and marketing firm that has continuously set industry track records since its inception in 1980.

In addition to his music and law enforcement interests, Bob Ham is also an authority on radio communications and firearms. As for the latter, he is currently a qualified Expert with both shotgun and submachine gun, and a qualified Master with the pistol and revolver. He occasionally competes in regional law enforcement competitions as a member of the Williamson County Sheriff's Department combat pistol team.

Licensed as an Advanced Class amateur radio operator, Bob is active on the amateur radio bands and has made thousands of radio contacts throughout the world. This hobby also affords him the opportunity to experiment with various types of antennas and electronic devices, including computers, packet radio, and radioteletype. This extensive hands-on knowledge in fire arms, law enforcement, electronics, and radio blends together to make Bob Ham's OVERLOAD series both entertaining and factual.

He currently resides in Brentwood, Tennessee, with his wife and children.

Fernando Cortes Hernandez was smiling. He had been dealt a setback, but he was back on the road to recovering his empire, and he would return to his throne, the gilded man. The smile vanishing, he rested a cheroot on his thin blood-less lips, snapped the 24-carat gold case shut and slipped the smokeholder inside his suit jacket. With a silver Ronson lighter he torched the cheroot, then ran well-manicured fingers over the lapel of his jacket, relished the exquisite cool touch of a thousand dollars' worth of Thai silk against his skin. He stared through the French double-doors. Beyond the lagoon, he saw the first golden rays of dawn jagging across the southern Florida sky. A pelican spread its wings and flapped over the lagoon. Six DEA agents, armed with assault rifles, patrolled the grounds beyond the ivy-trellised and palm-tree-fringed patio.

Death was coming in the eye of dawn, the man known as El Diablo thought, drawing the sweet cheroot smoke into his lungs. *And there will be fire in the sky*. The fire of the Devil.

Soon, El Diablo told himself, soon he would be a free man again. And the world would once more belong to him. The world and all its riches.

Death would bring him freedom. Shortly, he would get back to business as usual.

"Look at that guy, willya? Christ, the sight of him makes me sick. It's all I can do to keep from ripping his throat out with my bare hands."

Short but muscular, the swarthy, dark-haired Hernandez flexed his left hand, feeling the strength flow through his veins, his blood running hot with a burning hunger to be free. He wanted to laugh at the DEA agents. The tall, muscular agent named Stiles was losing badly at a game of spades. The shorter, heavyset Jameson chuckled each time he set his partner. Life was a game, after all, Hernandez decided. In his game, however, there were no winners—only survivors. And only one king of the mountain, one god of an empire that stretched around the world.

One conqueror.

Yes, Fernando Cortes Hernandez believed he was stronger, much, much stronger than any straight DEA man would ever be in a hundred lifetimes. Both physically and financially those agents of the DEA were impotent, he thought. They were men who dreamed of a drug-free world, dreamers, *sí*, who wanted to believe in the job they were doing. Blinded either by dreams, ambition, or their own smallness in a world they could never control, what they didn't want to see was that cocaine equalled big money.

Big, big *dinero*. The kind of money, Hernandez thought, and felt another tight grin stretch his lips, that God had. As long as politicians and law enforcement officers accepted a piece of the biggest action the world had ever seen, the world, and particularly *los Estados Unidos*, Fernando Cortes Hernandez knew, would never be drug-free. And he would keep on playing God.

Or the Devil. He was the one with the real power. The power of life and death:

"Relax, Big John. The Colombian's shit, we all know that. There's no sense getting your blood pressure pounding over him. I'd hate to see you have a heart attack right before the big day when we start to flush this piece of shit down the toilet. Besides," Jameson added, smiling, "you'd better get your mind back on this game of spades. At fifty cents a point, I'm up three hundred and twenty-five points."

They knew he could hear them, perhaps even wanted him to show anger over their barbs and cynical remarks. But they were as nothing to Fernando Cortes Hernandez. Indeed, they were less than the *campesinos* of his country. His cartel worth in excess of fifty billion dollars a year, worth far more than the 31.6 billion dollar GNP of his own country, Hernandez knew he could buy and sell them all a thousand times over. And if he couldn't buy and sell them like the dog meat they were, he thought, he could crush them like the worms they were.

"Look at this place, willya? A fancy mahogany bar in the corner of the room, loaded down with booze. A goddamn Jacuzzi in the living room. A stinkin' Olympic-sized pool out back. A bed with satin sheets for the drug-pushing shit. Cable television. We gotta keep the Colombian on ice in a palace that would make English royalty look like they were living in poverty."

"You know the routine, Big John," Hernandez heard Jameson sigh. "We've got to keep these hotshot Federal witnesses comfortable so they don't change their minds about singing. At least, that's the theory, anyway."

Hernandez kept smiling. He was used to style. And, he had to admit, the spacious, stone-and-marble mansion, secluded somewhere south of Miami, was indeed stylish. The DEA had broken their backs to make him comfortable. Then again, they had also broken their backs to extradite him from his ranchhouse outside of Medellin. Had he not been so burned out from four straight days of partying, the DEA men would never have caught him. Rule of thumb in the cocaine trade: Never get high on your own supply. But when a man is refining close to fifty tons of cocaine a month, he could afford to dip into his own supply, Hernandez thought. Hell, he could afford to shovel into the stuff.

"Only this snowbird may be snowing us about his big plea-bargaining routine," Stiles growled. "That Federal Witness Protection tag leaves a real bad taste in my mouth. For some reason, I got the feeling our boy here may just be buying time."

"For what?"

"I dunno. How should I know?"

Jameson smiled indulgently. "Take it easy, Big John. Remember, paranoia will destroy ya."

"Paranoia, huh? We've got twenty of our people and ten Miami vice cops toting M16s and submachine guns, assigned to protect the life of a cocaine vampire who calls himself the Devil," Stiles bitched. "And for what? So he can have his big day in a Miami court and walk away on some technicality? Plea-bargain his way back to Colombia? Maybe some judge who's got a nose-candy habit himself getting bought off by those big cocaine dollars? I'm not just paranoid, guy, I'm getting blind pissed-off just thinking about how these *coquitos* can twist, bend, and shit all over the system. And nobody seems to be able to do a damn thing about it. We nabbed him, sure, but the cocaine king is far from dead. If you ask me, all this beefed-up security may just be a sore thumb looking to get hacked off. And we're that thumb. Look at 'im," he said, jaw clenched, eyes burning at Hernandez. "Federal witness, my ass. Big songbird. Bullshit."

Jameson sighed. "How many death threats have been issued against our people this last week? Death threats that have been carried out, I'll remind you. Our agents overseas have been practically under siege since our people bagged and extradited Hernandez from Colombia," Jameson said. "Three agents shotgunned to death then hacked up in the street in Bogotá—a street full of witnesses, but nobody saw or heard a damn thing. Four more submachine-gunned in Bolivia. An agent in Panama shipped back to D.C. in bits and pieces. Now the hellstorm's blowing right across our own backyard—the family of a vice cop kidnapped and tortured to death right here in Miami."

"And you can bet we've got the sonofabitch behind it all," Stiles replied. "Right here, grinning from ear to ear, in our faces. Like he knows something we don't. I tell ya, either he bullshitted us about testifying or somebody down there is scared he might start pointing fingers to save his own skin."

Blowing smoke, Hernandez turned away from the French double doors. "You have a big mouth, *hombre*."

"What's that?" Stiles growled, and suddenly draped his hand over the stock of his M16. "You say something, shithead?"

"Relax, for chrissakes, will ya, John?" Jameson implored. "Get your hand off that M16 before you do something stupid."

"Stupid." Hernandez chuckled, then looked away from Stiles's burning gaze. "Stupid, perhaps. Bitter, *sí*. Simple, *sí*. Yours is a simple job for a simple mind. A simple man is often a bitter man, too. Simple life. Bitter ways. Dead-end life."

"I don't see how you quite figure all that

garbage about dead ends, Hernandez," Stiles said, his voice edged with anger. "You're the one who got caught with your lips locked on a crack pipe and dragged out of Colombia."

"The world," Hernandez said, solemnly gazing at the guards near the patio, "is a whore, and you must indulge her. The sooner you learn that . . . the better off you'll be."

Stiles grinned at Jameson. "The world's a whore? Now what's that—"

Suddenly, the DEA agents froze, locked gazes. The cards slipped out of Stiles's hand.

The throbbing seemed to descend right on top of the safe house.

"Are we expecting company?" Stiles rasped, snatching up his M16. "That's a chopper! Nobody told me anything—"

The sounds of autofire, screams lanced through the windows of the room.

Looking skyward, Hernandez smiled, his eyes lit with grim anticipation. He flicked his cheroot aside as the French Aerospatiale Alouette swooped from the murky sky. A split second later, as the DEA agents opened up on the converted gunship with a barrage of M16 autofire, the chopper turned the stygian gloom ablaze.

Fire ripped the dawn sky asunder.

A glowing tongue of white phosphorous fire spewed from the long nozzle on the gunship's nose. Shrieks ripped the air, and M16s went silent as the DEA agents burst into human torches. Flaming demons crashed through the trellis, wrapped in slick-looking sheets of fire. A wave of flames consumed the patio, devouring plants and human life alike.

A demon danced in front of the French double doors. Flailing, he tumbled through those doors, wailing like a banshee. Glass shards razored past Hernandez, who held his ground. Silently, he dared the fickle gods of fate to hurt him.

"Jesus Christ!" Stiles gasped, freezing in his tracks for a second, his face cut with horror and shock as the blood curdling screams filled the room. "We're being hit! What the hell's—"

Hernandez then saw the dark shadows pouring out of the woods. Automatic weapons chattered in their fists, spewing hot lead over the stunned DEA agents.

"You sonofabitch! You planned this whole thing! You set us up!"

Hernandez whirled. There was murderous rage in Stiles's eyes. For a moment, the cocaine czar would have sworn that Stiles was going to cut him down in cold blood.

"John! John!"

The demon's screams died. The stench of roasting flesh pierced Hernandez's nose. It was a good smell, he thought. The cleansing fire. The corpse was the charred, shriveled symbol of the moral decay of the United States.

Then Hernandez saw the pencil-tip flame spitting from the muzzle of Jameson's M16.

Stiles cried out, a line of 5.56mm slugs marching up the backs of his legs. As Stiles crumpled to the floor, Hernandez scooped up the fallen M16. For a stretched second, Hernandez and Jameson stared at each other.

Teeth gnashing, Stiles grabbed at his legs, rolling around in a growing puddle of his own blood.

Hernandez smiled at Jameson. The furious din of autofire crushed in on the safe house.

"So I am a piece of *mierda*, eh, *hombre?*"

Jameson shrugged, appearing apologetic. "C'mon, give me a break. I had to make it sound convincing."

"No . . . no." Stiles looked up at Jameson, his eyes burning with hatred. "Not you. Not—"

"Finish him, *hombre*."

Regret flashed through Jameson's eyes. He looked down at Stiles. "Sorry, Big John. What can I tell you? I got caught in a tangled web."

Without hesitation, Jameson drilled a 3-round burst into Stiles's chest.

The gunship lowered to the ground beyond the shattered French double doors. Rotor wash hurled chips of glass against Hernandez. His gaze narrowed against the glass shrapnel, Hernandez told Jameson, "Your information had better be good, *hombre*. Or you will not live to see the sun set. *Comprende?*"

The smoking M16 was lowered to Jameson's side. "It's good. I wouldn't risk my ass like this if it weren't."

Hernandez grunted.

There was a commotion behind Jameson.

Three swarthy men surged through the doorway. With long strides, Hernandez moved toward his soldiers. They toted Argentine FMK-3 submachine guns. Hernandez smiled. There was no mistaking his *segundo* and top assassin, Raul El Leon Pizarro. Six and a half feet tall, with shoulder-length hair as black as coal and an eyepatch over his left eye, Pizarro, Hernandez knew, could put fear into the heart of the toughest of *hombres*. There was a huge machete sheathed in black leather at Pizarro's side. More than once, Hernandez had seen El Leon hack the arms or legs off an enemy and feed the bloody stump to a caiman.

"Fernando," Pizarro greeted, and the two men hugged each other. "I knew we would see each other again."

"Once again, Raul, you have shown you have the courage of a lion."

"They were nothing. The place is surrounded. All of the DEA men are dead. Another helicopter is on the way now to lift us out."

"Good, good. We must leave now. Quickly."

Suspiciously, Pizarro looked at Jameson. "Wait a minute, Fernando. What about him?"

"Him? Do not forget—that *gringo* has the masterlist, Raul. He lives . . . for now." A cruel smile then stretched the cocaine czar's lips as he looked at the body of Stiles. "Let us see, though, if he has the stomach for what may lie ahead in the days to come for his DEA *amigos*. Give our new addition to the New Conquistadors your machete, Raul."

Jameson tensed, as Pizarro slid the machete from its sheath. "Wh-what . . ."

"Be quick about it, *hombre*," Hernandez snapped at Jameson. "Raul, you watch him and make sure he does admirable work. If he hesitates, kill him. Sometimes they vomit over such work. Should he vomit, kill him."

Jameson looked at the machete as if it were some contagious virus.

"Take it!" Hernandez barked.

Trembling, Jameson took the machete. "Wh-what . . . what do you want me to do with it?"

Hernandez smiled. "You are to make Big John not so big, *hombre*, that's what."

El Diablo laughed.

It was back to business as usual.

The statistics were frightening.

The newspaper headlines were horrifying.

The world had gone mad.

Vic Gabriel felt his teeth set on edge. Expelling a pent-up breath, he looked up from the *Washington Post*. Beneath Gabriel was a glaring headline about the massacre of DEA agents and Miami vice detectives at a safe house in Dade County, a hit that had gone down because of the extradition of a drug baron from Colombia. Another major supplier of cocaine, who had also been extradited recently from Colombia, had been quoted in the article Gabriel had just read: *Cocaine will be the atom bomb that destroys the United States*.

The sonofabitch had that right, Gabriel thought, and felt the bitterness eating away at his guts.

Cocaine had killed his younger brother, Jim, years ago.

Following his brother's death, Vic Gabriel had launched a short but explosive war against the death pushers, up and down the East Coast. During that war, Gabriel had found a close ally within the Drug Enforcement Administration. That agent, Bob Jeffreys, had sympathized with Gabriel and put his job, and his life, on the line for the man in the belief that fire had to be fought with fire. For days now, Gabriel had been poring over and mentally chewing up the intelligence Jeffreys had air-expressed to him from across the Atlantic Ocean. The statistics were enough to send someone reeling in disbelief. More than two billion dollars of cocaine was squeezed into Florida alone every week. And that, according to the agent's intel, was a conservative estimate . . . a very conservative estimate. It was reported that only one in every nine hauls of cocaine was seized by law enforcement officials. Tons of cocaine were stockpiled in refineries in Colombia, Bolivia, Peru, and other South American countries. Plenty of the black snow, Gabriel thought, to replace any load that was confiscated. The DEA and other law enforcement agencies simply didn't have the manpower or the money to win the war against the *narcotraficantes*. It was the drug barons who had all the money, all the manpower. And they never hesitated to flex muscle when and wherever necessary to get what they wanted.

Shaking a Marlboro free from a rumpled pack, Gabriel flicked a gold-plated Zippo, torched the smoke. Engraved on the Zippo was *7th SFG— No compromise*. The Zippo was a memento from his father, Colonel Charles Gabriel, who had helped in the conception of the Special Forces in 1952.

Vic Gabriel himself was ex–Special Forces. He was also a former assassin for the CIA's Special Operations Division. It was because of the CIA that Vic Gabriel and the other three commandos of Eagle Force were forced to set up a new base of operations in the Pyrenees along the French–Spanish border. Eagle Force's last mission, a killhunt against the Soviet SPETSNAZ up the icy slopes of Mount Makalu in Nepal, had also locked them in the death sights of a CIA execution squad. After that mission, Eagle Force had wiped out the rest of that Company hit team in the Florida Everglades. Used as expendables by the CIA for a mission that had resulted in failure in Nepal, Eagle Force knew that the CIA would never give up the hunt to terminate them now. With the large sum of money they had managed to stash in a Swiss bank account after their first mission, the commandos of Eagle Force had bought out and set up their war base in a château, high up in the Pyrenees. Like any number of the ten thousand other châteaus in France, Gabriel's war base was originally built back in the Dark Ages to protect landowners from the barbarian hordes of Franks, Visigoths, and Burgundians. Vic Gabriel found grim irony in that. He knew there was really no safe place, no protection anywhere in the world from the savage hordes of animal man.